THE DEAD BUTLER CAPER

THE
DEAD BUTLER CAPER

FRANK NORMAN

MACDONALD AND JANE'S · LONDON

First published in Great Britain in 1978 by
Macdonald and Jane's Publishers Limited,
Paulton House, 8 Shepherdess Walk, London N.1.

Copyright © Frank Norman 1978

ISBN 0 354 04258 0

Photoset, printed and bound
in Great Britain by
REDWOOD BURN LIMITED
Trowbridge & Esher

TO
MARGARET FITZHERBERT

CHAPTER ONE

Black Satin Hotpants had a wiggle that could fry a man's eyeballs at fifty yards. She was a sizzling little hooker just the right side of the age of consent, and only too well aware of the fortune to be made from the meter that ticked away in her knickers. She plied for hire, on wicked pencil-thin high-heels, on a short stretch of pavement between Piccadilly underground station and the first set of traffic lights in the Haymarket. The view from my third-floor office window in Regent Chambers exactly overlooked the limits of her beat. Watching Black Satin Hotpants mincing up and down was not, however, without discomfort. All but the bottom six inches of my window was blocked off by a giant hoarding that advertised Hankey Bannister's Scotch whisky and it was only by adopting a position of prayer that I was able to catch a glimpse of her. Business had been slack of late and ogling Hotpants had given me housemaid's knee.

I was deeply immersed in my favourite fantasy when miraculously the phone rang. There is of course nothing miraculous about a phone ringing and, in normal circumstances, I wouldn't've given it a second thought, but I'd not paid the bill for six months and the telephone company had, hardheartedly, though understandably, disconnected my line a fortnight ago — the computer must've gone on the blink. I clambered to my feet, limped across the room, and cautiously lifted the receiver.

I recognized the mellifluous cadences of Prudence Pride on the line and the air wheezed out of the leather upholstery, like a mighty sigh, as I sank heavily into the battered swivel chair behind my desk.

'Ed Nelson,' she cried. 'Something unspeakably awful has happened. Can you come round to Sammy's place instantly?'

'Do me a favour,' I replied wearily. 'I've never done anything instantly in my life.'

1

Pru did her nut. Doing her nut in order to get her own way was Pru's speciality.

'Call yourself a private investigator,' she shrilled hysterically. 'You couldn't investigate your way out of a wet paper bag.'

I said: 'That's a very cruel thing to say.'

'If you're not in this house within the next half hour you're fired!'

She knew to a nicety how to get people rattled. In abnormal circumstances I'd've undoubtedly told her to get stuffed, but circumstances were normal. I was skint as a church mouse and Pru was my one and only client. I needed the 20 quid a day plus expenses and mileage that she'd been bunging me for the past three weeks for spying on her lover's wife.

It was Pru who'd engaged my services, but I was pretty sure it was her boyfriend, Sir Samford Peveril, who shelled out the crisp fivers in settlement of my weekly account. I'd not so far had the pleasure of meeting him personally, but a swift butchers at Debrett had revealed the following information:

SAMFORD HAMILTON JAMES PEVERIL
22nd Baronet; *b.* December 9th, 1929; *ed.* at Eton, and at Balliol Coll., Oxford; Major Coldstream Guards 1949/54; Korean War 1950/53; awarded MC, DSO 1951/2: *m.* Sonia Clevenhall-Folkes, *da.* 2nd Earl of Clevenhall.
Seat. Bramley Hall, Bramley, Wiltshire.
Clubs. White's and Boodles.

To the left of the entry was the Peveril crest: Two eagles looking daggers at a stag, and beneath it was the family motto: 'Mind How You Go.' With all that going for him it was not altogether surprising that he preferred to remain in the background.

If Pru was to be believed, his wife, Lady Sonia, was having it off something rotten with a family friend by the name of Patrick Tomlinson. Pru had indicated that if I could dig up enough dirt that would stick in court there was a better than even chance that she would be able to persuade her high-born boyfriend to file for divorce and thus leave the way clear for her to commit matrimony with him and step daintily into his ex-wife's shoes.

It would be somewhat less than kind to suggest that Pru's sole

2

interest lay in gaining a title, money and a fair-sized estate in Wiltshire, on which stood Bramley Hall, the country seat of the Peveril family for more than three centuries. It was faintly possible that she loved him as much as he appeared to love her, but that is the kind of thing that one can never be quite certain about.

'Did you hear what I said, Mr Nelson?' she snapped.

'Keep your hair on,' I grunted and hung up.

The Peveril town house off Belgrave Square was the kind of property that a working-class pools winner might pay through the nose for if his wife got ideas above her station. Pru had given me the address for my files, but this was the first time that I'd been invited around. A quick appraisal told me that the bricklayers got to work sometime during the early part of the nineteenth century; the marble cupola off to one side of the roof indicated that the original architect had been influenced by the mathematical convictions of Palladio. The pillared portico at the front of the house induced a passing thought that Nash had at sometime influenced the gerrybuilder – not bad going for a man who smokes and drinks a lot and has a very limited knowledge of architecture.

Parked outside on a double yellow line was Pru's orange Lamborghini. I didn't much relish the prospect of our imminent encounter. Pru had the kind of disposition that got on my wick. It was second nature to her to turn the mildest conversation into a blazing row, the meekest criticism into a wounding insult and the most innocent lunch date into a passionate affair. But there could be no denying that she was as darkly beautiful as she was neurotic – her blue-black hair, gleaming like a raven's wing, cascaded over her shoulders in a riot of natural curls framing her oval face. Her full red lips revealed white even teeth when she smiled and a sharp acquiline nose gave her a perpetual air of haughty disdain. She had the glamorous silhouette of a fashion model, and her clothes bore that costly stamp of elegance which is the hall-mark of exclusive haute-couture. I knew little about her except that at twenty-five years of age she already had a reputation in sophisticated society that could hardly've been rivalled by Anne-Marie-Louise d'Orléans at the Court of Louis XIV.

3

I plunged my hands into the pockets of my battered old gabardine trenchcoat, sighed audibly and trotted up the half dozen stone steps to the iron-studded front door. To my surprise and mild irritation, no one came to the door when I pressed the bell. I jabbed it a second time more urgently. This too brought no response so I beat out a rapid tattoo with the hefty brass knocker, stepped back a couple of paces, and looked up at the house just in time to see a curtain flutter in an upstairs window.

'Now what?' I muttered, and knocked and rang simultaneously.

The door opened slightly and I tumbled that someone had left the catch off. I pushed it the rest of the way, gingerly, with the toe of my shoe and peered inside. The richly carpeted passage, hung with family portraits, that led to the rooms at the back of the house was brightly lit by a crystal chandelier, entirely deserted and still as the grave.

I called: 'Anyone home?' and stepped over the threshold.

There was no reply.

I made my way, cautiously, a short distance along the passage.

'Miss Pride. It's Ed Nelson, Miss Pride!'

Still no reply.

I had reached the first of the doors along the passage. It was slightly ajar. I tapped lightly with my finger tips then pushed it open with the flat of my hand. The room was sumptuously furnished; I entered stealthily and glanced about. There was an elegant glass-fronted rosewood cabinet against one wall, quite empty apart from a broken tea cup. A heavy bookcase, festooned with finely-tooled bindings, towered to the ceiling to my right. The rest of the furniture was lavishly decorated with ormolu sphinxes and leering griffins and over the mantelpiece hung an indelicate Boucher. Lumpishly on the floor by the fireplace, formally attired in morning coat and striped trousers, was a bulky corpse. What had once been a face was beaten to pulp. Congealed blood and fragments of flesh were splattered over the wall and surrounding area as thickly as oil paint on a Jackson Pollock canvas. Not a pretty sight. I reeled backwards as though someone had wafted an income tax demand under my nose and clutched at an elegant giltwood chair for support.

4

'Stone the crows,' I gasped and, with what little I had left in the way of legs, flung out of the room. I collided head on with Prudence Pride as she came dashing along the passage in the direction of the front door, clutching a vanity case. She fell away from me and covered her right eye with her left hand.

'Clumsy clot,' she bleated. 'You've probably given me a black eye.'

'Black eye!' I jerked a thumb over my shoulder. 'There's a colourful scene in there, that'll give you a bloody sight more than a black eye.'

She dropped her vanity case and clutched my arm.

'Ed, you've simply got to help me.' Her ruby lips trembled and she lamped me with beseeching eyes. 'Sammy isn't here and I don't know what's happened. It's Mrs Brown's afternoon off... no one knows yet except you and me. I was absolutely frantic. I didn't know who to call... and then I thought of you. You won't let me down, will you, Ed?'

She squeezed my arm remorselessly and batted her eyelashes to underline the appeal. I'm a sucker when it comes to holding out a helping hand to ladies in distress. I can refuse them nothing – but I'd just as soon they didn't ask me.

'Depends just how far you want me to stick my neck out. I take it that you haven't called the rozzers?'

'No, no,' she cried. 'No one must know I was here. I owe it to Sammy. It's going to be terrible for him dealing with this frightful... this senseless... murder.' She could hardly mouth the word. 'Without me being dragged into it, and embarrassing questions being asked about our relationship.'

'But what about that poor stiff in there? He looks like he got on the wrong side of Boris Karloff.'

'It's Parkhurst, the butler, a hateful man... but it's unbelievable that he's dead, like that, and nobody here. Oh – what are we to do?' She shivered and her thin silk dress rustled like a shuffle of cards.

'Where is Samford anyway?' I asked, beginning to be practical.

'I don't know... I don't know,' she wailed. 'He was taking me to lunch at the Ritz but he just didn't turn up... or phone, or anything. I popped around to see if he was here and had forgotten. But there wasn't anyone and then I found ...'

She buried her face in her hands, the way girls do when they're upset or want to hide their feelings. I massaged my arm where her vice-like grip had temporarily suspended circulation.

'You don't suppose he's done a bunk?'

She raised her face from her hands. Her eyes blazed at me.

'Samford could never ... you don't think he ... no, no he would never ... you bastard!'

'Well, who did it then?'

'Burglars!'

'Burglars?' I echoed incredulously.

'That's right,' she rasped. 'Those men who break into people's houses and steal things.'

'I know what burglars are,' I assured her. 'I'm acquainted with several personally. Family men mostly, devoted to their wives and children. Not one of them would use violence in the furtherance of a crime.'

'I suppose the next thing you'll suggest is that I had something to do with it!' She was on the verge of hysterics.

'Perish the thought,' I said, then added for safety's sake. 'Well, did you?'

She let out a strangled cry of anguish, picked up her vanity case and, waving it about threateningly, she fled from the house. She paused on the doorstep for an instant, looked back at me nervously and said: 'You won't tell the police I was here will you, Ed? I'll ring you.'

Then she plunged out of sight and moments later her sexy Lamborghini roared off down the street.

A second look at Parkhurst's body convinced me that Pru had made a double-shrewd move in making herself scarce – it crossed my mind that I should do the same. But it was too late for that. Even the most muddle-headed police investigation would reveal my connection with Sir Samford and I had, in any case, left a generous supply of my dabs about the place. There was nothing for it but to phone Scotland Yard.

CHAPTER TWO

While waiting for the law to put in an appearance I idled away my time sniffing out clues. At the scene of a murder anything and everything can turn out to be a clue to the identity of the killer: a blonde hair on the arm rest of a sofa, a lipstick-smeared cigarette butt in the ashtray, a muddy footprint on the drawing-room carpet, anything at all. An investigator must be fanatically suspicious and always on the lookout for the unexpected. Why is the coal skuttle full of chicken feathers? Why is the corpse wearing a crash helmet, football boots and purple satin pyjamas? It's attention to the minutest detail that ties up the loose ends in a murder investigation. So they say, and they may well be right. I only have other people's word to go on here. Despite the fact that a brass plaque engraved: 'EDWARD NELSON. PRIVATE INVESTIGATOR' is screwed to my office door (a waste of a tenner that could've been more usefully wasted on Hankey Bannister's whisky) murder is out of my class.

Detective agencies, if you scan the Yellow Pages, are offering all kinds of technological specialities these days like de-bugging, electronic screening, international surveillance and counter industrial espionage. But I'm a man who knows his limitations. I'm an old-fashioned divorce snooper, process server and all-round bearer of bad tidings. Now and then I get a little fresh air and exercise by tracking down some young chick who's bolted with her boyfriend. I'm on Christian-name terms with a number of bad faces in the underworld, and insurance companies occasionally ask me to spread the word that there's a handsome reward being offered and no questions asked, for the return of certain shiny items of sentimental value to dukes and earls. But I never get above my station. A pal of mine, in the same line of business, stepped out of his class a year or two back and ended up on the mortuary slab. He cornered a gangland killer in a dark alley and came off second best with a bullet between his eyes. I never did find out what it was all about and I didn't ask.

Since I had to hang around the premises in which someone, loosely connected with my client, had snuffed it, I decided to have a casual butchers around.

A cursory inspection revealed a number of things of riveting interest. Next to the drawing-room was the library and it struck me as decidedly odd that half the books had been pulled from their shelves and scattered around the floor. It crossed my mind that the murderer had carried out an untidy search, but a closer examination revealed that many of the spines were broken. Extensive damage of this kind was not in keeping with the books having simply fallen to the floor — I deduced that an illiterate maniac had been showing his resentment at never having learnt to read.

Up in the master bedroom a naked Italian peasant woman lay voluptuously on the four poster bed. She'd been done in oils sometime during the last century and was elegantly framed in gilt. Over the mantelpiece, where I guessed she usually hung, the door of the wall safe swung listlessly on its hinges like a limp wrist. It was as bare as Mother Hubbard's cupboard and scattered around the floor were several bundles of legal documents, tied with red tape, and a number of empty jewel cases.

I picked up one or two for closer inspection and, while I was admiring the pig skin and ruffled satin interiors that went with inscriptions such as Cartier, Van Cleef and Arpels and Harry Winston, a piercing scream split my ear drums.

I got to the head of the stairs in time to see a plump middle-aged woman in a flowered pinafore plunge across the hall screaming like a banshee. She disappeared through a green baize door that presumably led to the basement. She kept up the racket all the way, though it was nicely muffled as the baize door swung to behind her.

Finding a strange man in the house would no doubt give her a nasty turn, especially if she leapt to the conclusion that he was the same bloke responsible for the unpleasant mess she'd unexpectedly stumbled on in the drawing room. Nevertheless I followed her into the basement. My best efforts to calm her down got nowhere. Ten minutes and fifteen outbursts of violent hysteria later, I stumbled out into the basement area, lit a cigarette and glanced upwards.

There towering above me on the front doorstep was Superintendent Bernard Clews, jabbing irritably at the door bell. The Super was a tall man with iron-grey hair, steely blue eyes and a big nose, beneath which he sported a clipped military moustache. He was the tallest man of not more than fifty-seven I'd ever met. The distance between his size thirteen boots and the top of his head was exactly six feet five and three-quarter inches; his trilby hat made him two inches taller. His great height, moustache and trilby apart, he looked more than a little like Sherlock Holmes.

Detective Sergeant Algernon du Ponte, Superintendent Clews' assistant, was a thirty-eight-year-old university graduate of average height, but up against his boss he looked like a Lilliputian. A less well-bred young man would probably have suffered from an inferiority complex at being towered over for most of his waking hours. But, far from feeling inferior, Sergeant du Ponte was devoted to the Super and proud to be his right-hand man. Clews, who had not even managed to scrape into grammar school, was for his part daunted by his sergeant's refined accent and university degree. Nonetheless they were an indomitable duo, respected and feared by the underworld and held in the highest esteem by the Commissioner.

I put the fore-finger and little finger of my left hand under my tongue and whistled.

'Down here, Super,' I called. 'I'm down here in the basement.'

He glanced down at me sharply.

'Ed Nelson! What the hell are you doing down there?'

'Waiting for a number nineteen bus,' I replied and clambered up the stone steps to street level. 'Thought I'd better hang about 'til you showed up,' I said as I came abreast of the lofty investigator and his assistant.

'Extremely sensible, what?' said du Ponte.

Algernon du Ponte invariably tacked a speculative 'what' on the end of everything he said. It was an unconscious affectation that he'd picked up from his eccentric old tutor during university days.

The Superintendent gave me a fatherly smile.

'Bit off your usual patch aren't you, Ed?' he said.

I smiled apprehensively.

'A job's a job,' I shrugged.

'I'm never surprised to see you hanging around Soho street corners and underworld dives,' Clews commented. 'But business must certainly be looking up if the upper crust are competing to retain your services.'

'I'm not fussy who I work for,' I replied coolly. 'Don't you want to go inside and take a gander at the *corpus delicti*? It's a real humdinger.'

I led the way down the basement steps and the CID followed behind.

As we entered the house through the servants' entrance, the good Mrs Brown, whom I'd left untidily on a kitchen chair, came back to life. Another of her screams rent the air.

Algernon was experienced with servants. He slapped her smartly on both cheeks and showed her his police card at the same time. It did the trick, she sat bolt upright and paid attention.

'Where's the body?' asked Clews.

I pointed at the ceiling, then led the way upstairs.

'Not a pleasant sight,' said Clews as he looked upon Parkhurst's mutilated countenance.

Du Ponte stood next to him, stiff from shock, his face white as paper.

'Don't just stand there, sergeant,' ordered Clews. 'Get on to forensic and call an ambulance.'

The detective sergeant dragged his eyes from the gory spectacle and staggered blindly across the room. He reached the bay windows, turned on his heel and looked frantically about.

'Where's the phone?' he groaned.

'There's one in the hall,' I told him.

He grunted and retraced his steps across the room. I ambled over to where Clews was standing, took a packet of cigarettes from my jacket pocket and offered him one.

'No thanks,' he said, not looking my way. 'Given up.'

'You used to be a chain smoker,' I said in amazement.

Algernon's toffy-nosed cadences drifted in from the hall.

'What's that you say? . . . The Savoy hotel? . . . I want the Yard . . . Scotland Yard! Oh dear, frightfully sorry, I must have misdialled . . . Do please forgive me, so sorry to have troubled you.' The bell tinkled as he rang off and Clews and I exchanged an involuntary smile.

'Extension twenty-eight,' du Ponte said a moment or two

later, then after a short pause: 'Charlie, would you alert Professor Green-Parker.... Yes, that's right, we shall certainly be needing the murder bag ... number twenty-five.... Yes, yes, the whole works. Whoever's on duty in the fingerprint department and a photographer.... Soon as you can, old chap.' He rang off and came back into the room. Clews glanced at him.

'Get through all right?' he asked.

Algernon blushed.

'The team are on their way, sir.'

'Splendid,' Clews said. 'Find something to cover up that poor man's head. Then go down to the kitchen and see if you can get anything out of the help.'

He pointed a finger in my direction, 'You come with me.'

'Right away, Super,' I said.

'Now!' he snapped.

Feeling more than a little ill at ease, I jabbed a fag aggressively into the corner of my mouth and obediently trotted after him as he strode out of the room in his seven-league boots. In the hall he came to an abrupt halt and swung round on me, unsnapping his notebook.

'Right, Ed,' he said softly. 'I shall have to ask for your full co-operation on this one.'

I gave him a sickly smile.

'Always a pleasure to help the police.'

'I take it the deceased was the butler. Can you give me the full name of the owner of this house?'

'Sir Samford Peveril, 22nd Baronet.'

'Spelling?'

'P-E-V-E-R-I-L.'

'Not two L's?' he said, writing.

'No.'

'Age and occupation?'

'About fifty or so. Man of means. Don't think he goes in for occupation much.'

'Anyone else live here? Wife, children, anything like that?'

I put a finger and thumb to my temples. After a moment, I glanced at my watch, puffed on my fag and said:

'Childless marriage, as far as I know. His wife Lady Sonia

11

stays here when she's in town, I believe. But they've a country place in Wiltshire, Bramley Hall.'

'Right. That'll do for now,' he said and gave me one of those penetrating glares cops specialize in – to the acute discomfort of suspects. I knew he hadn't finished with me yet, not by a long chalk.

'Righto, Ed. What exactly were you doing here?'

I ought to have been ready for an obvious question like that.

'Just happened to be passing and thought I'd look in.'

'Did you have an appointment?'

'Not exactly.'

'Why did you come around then?'

'To give my client a progress report on my investigations.'

'Working for Sir Samford?'

'I'm afraid I cannot reveal that,' I replied cautiously.

'Some sort of marital love tangle going on, is there?'

'I'm not at liberty to . . .'

'. . . Never mind,' he cut in sharply. 'You've turned the house over of course.'

'I had a look round.'

'Find anything?'

I said: 'It looks as though there's been a bundle in the library, and the peter's been cleaned out in the bedroom.'

'Hmm,' he sniffed. 'There was no one here when you arrived?'

I crossed my fingers behind my back.

'No.'

'You're sure about that?'

'Didn't see anyone,' I replied boldly. 'Except for the old biddy downstairs, but she didn't show up until after I called you.'

Clews turned on another of his penetrating looks.

'I just wouldn't want to find out that you've been keeping things from me, Ed,' he said gently.

I mustered an expression of mortification.

'Would I lie to you, Super?'

'You say the housekeeper wasn't here when you arrived?'

'That's right.'

He pounced: 'Who let you in then?'

I blanched: 'Front door was open.'

'Always go barging into the houses of the nobility when you

find the door "ajar", eh?' He was turning nasty.

Algernon du Ponte appeared at the drawing-room door brandishing a heavy service revolver.

'Do you have a moment, sir?' he asked. 'I may have stumbled upon something of interest, what?'

'For God's sake, du Ponte,' cried Clews. 'Don't point that thing at me.'

'Damn fine cannon, what?' The sergeant sniffed the muzzle. 'Been fired recently – in the last hour or two I'd say.'

The Superintendent hurried across the hall. I followed close on his heels.

'Where did you find it, exactly?'

Algernon pointed the revolver across the room.

'In the drawer of that little rosewood *escritoire*, sir.'

'Funny place to keep a shooter,' I volunteered and craned my neck to inspect the firearm more closely. 'Smith and Wesson 44 Magnum – the most powerful handgun in the world.'

'Tell you what, Ed,' said Clews. 'Why don't you just trot along and leave us to muddle through in our own laborious way?'

'Only trying to help,' I grinned.

'I shall expect you round at the Yard first thing in the morning to make a full statement.'

'First thing?'

'Not later than ten.'

'I'll get an alarm call.'

As I stepped out of the front door an ambulance and a police car came sirening nose to tail round the corner, and skidded to a tyre-smoking halt outside the house. All four doors of the police car flew open like switch-blades and half a dozen forensic experts spilled out onto the pavement.

Propping up a lamp post on the other side of the road was a tearaway in a heavily upholstered overcoat. I didn't like the look of things at all. Inwardly cursing Pru, I resolved to duck out of this affair at the first opportunity.

CHAPTER THREE

At variance with the tough wording of my lease, the Haymarket office doubled as my place of business and bedroom. It seemed a criminal waste of money to rent a place to sleep when there was a serviceable horsehair sofa in the office. Of course, if the flint-hearted agent for the Nassau-based property company that owned the building ever twigged that I shaved, brushed my teeth and rinsed my underwear on the premises he'd have me out on my ear. But so long as the rent got paid there was no reason for him to take an interest in my life-style so, for the time being at least, I had provided myself with what the police call a 'fixed abode'.

It was two in the morning. The neon lights of Piccadilly Circus winked all the colours of the rainbow through my unshaded window. Naked except for Y-fronts I stretched out on the rock-hard sofa, covered myself with a candy-striped goose-down continental quilt (that I'd picked up dirt cheap at a department store sale) and fell to thinking things over. The early editions of the linens were probably on the street already. And none but *The Times* would pass up the heaven-sent opportunity of titillating their flagging readership. Banner headlines flashed across my mind's eye: BELGRAVIA BUTLER SKULL BASHED IN. BARONET'S SERVANT SLAIN. PEVERIL MENIAL MURDERED . . . Suddenly, for the second time in less than twenty-four hours, the phone rang. I sprang off the sofa and padded barefoot across the room.

I put the receiver to my ear. A man's voice came on the line. He spoke rapidly in a voice trembling with excitement.

'I've seen your advert in the newsagent's window – the one in St Martin's Lane. I want you to give me the most unbelievable experience.' He hesitated for an instant. 'What exactly is the "unbelievable experience" you mention in your ad? I don't want to come unless it really is *unbelievable* – I'm sick of short times.'

'Whatever turns you on, mate,' I said.

The line went dead. Having a similar number to a prostitute is one of the hazards of living in Piccadilly. Oddball punters got through to me at least twice a week. I left the phone off the hook and crumpled onto the sofa like a discarded Kleenex.

14

The headlines that I'd foreseen duly appeared the following morning. They were accompanied by flattering snapshots from the Peveril family album. One flagging tabloid, anticipating the increased circulation that could be derived from a touch of outrageous sensationalism, had already christened Parkhurst's bloody demise 'THE CASE OF THE BATTERED BUTLER' and promised their readers a day-by-day progress report on the investigation plus the low-down on the high-born Peveril dynasty. They also mentioned in passing that a load of valuable tom had gone missing.

I noted that no one had yet succeeded in contacting Sir Samford. Though there were several hysterical quotes from Lady Sonia who was said to be doing her nut about the whole affair down at the ancestral home in Wiltshire.

Mrs Brown was also wallowing in her hour of glory. She leered from the tabloids, still in her pinafore; she was quite 'done up' and round at her sister-in-law's. The master had told her he was going out to lunch and she'd left the house at 12 o'clock to do a spot of window shopping in Oxford Street: '. . . it being her afternoon off, like.'

'It'd be ever so nice to get back early,' she'd told herself. 'What with her Ladyship saying she might be popping up from the country to see the new Harold Pinter play at the National Theatre – very fond of a night out on the town her Ladyship is.'

After taking her hat and coat off (a nice little feather toque she'd bought in a sale – the mind boggled) she'd spent a penny, then popped upstairs to find Mr Parkhurst and ask him if her Ladyship was still expected. After that the story got quite familiar. Fortunately, what with her 'having such a turn' at having to recount the gory details of finding the body, the sinister private eye who'd been prowling around the house was quite unrecognizable. Du Ponte, on the other hand, had impressed her. He was 'quite the gentleman'.

Superintendent Clews was immune to the antics of the press. My interview with him was conducted with brittle efficiency and the sticky statement that I signed was only inaccurate by omission. I left Prudence Pride out of it.

Clews did not betray whether or not he believed a word of it. But you don't have to take the oath before signing a statement

15

so if he tried to do me for perjury a good lawyer might be able to get me off on the grounds that I had an unhappy childhood and suffered from dizzy spells and lapses of memory whenever I came into contact with girls.

I got as much mileage as I could out of the confidentiality I owed my clients. While intimating that it might've been Sir Samford who hired me, I hinted that it was remotely possible that Lady Sonia was having it off something rotten with a rough-trade fortune hunter. Du Ponte got down the flannel in a legible hand.

Once I'd reached the events of the preceding afternoon, I was on firmer ground and, apart from not mentioning the darkly seductive temptress I'd bumped into in the hall, I told it the way it happened.

Pru was waiting on my doorstep when I got back to the office and I was eager to collect *anything* she was prepared to do for me for keeping her name out of it.

'I've been waiting here for simply ages,' she scolded as I fumbled for my latch key.

I smiled goodnaturedly.

'How many?'

'Too many.' She followed me into the office. 'Where have you been anyway.'

'Down the nick to make a statement.'

She bit her lower lip and her eyes registered panic.

'You didn't tell . . . ?' she faltered.

'No.'

She breathed a sign of relief and slumped onto the sofa.

'I suppose you don't happen to have such a thing as a drink?'

I yanked open the bottom drawer of the desk and took out a two-thirds empty bottle of Hankey Bannister's Scotch whisky, and a couple of plastic cups.

'Ugh!' she cried. 'Plastic cups.'

'Whisky will get you drunk whatever you drink it out of,' I said attempting gaiety and slopped three fingers into each of the cups. 'Water?'

'No thanks.'

The drink seemed to steady her nerves a little. Her face was dead and impassive like a wooden mask: 'Have the police interviewed Sammy yet?'

'Not as far as I know. He's still on the missing list.'

'Oh, Ed . . .' She half sobbed. 'Where is he? What can have happened to him? I was sure that he'd ring me. He wouldn't turn to anyone else if he was in trouble. So I just sat by the telephone all night. I waited and waited . . . but it didn't ring. He hasn't called me since the day before yesterday. He stood me up for lunch – and he's never even been five minutes late for a date before. Oh Ed, what can have happened to him and what are the police going to think if he doesn't come forward?'

I bit back the obvious answer.

'Don't fall to bits,' I advised. 'Drink up. Perhaps he's been run over by a bus and is languishing in hospital somewhere with amnesia.'

'Don't even say such a thing,' she shrieked and fell back, with majestic slowness, on the sofa, closing her blue eye-lids and letting her well-developed mammaries heave with emotion.

I poured myself another slug of whisky and sat feasting my eyes on her. She was miles the best-looking client I'd ever had and I fancied her double strong. She was the kind of girl that kings gave up thrones for, millionaires smothered in diamonds and mink, and clapped-out private detectives got nowhere with.

Her eyelids fluttered open after a while. There wasn't much colour in her cheeks and the wooden expression had returned.

'Something mysterious and terrifying has happened,' a hoarse whisper informed me.

'Too damn right. Parkhurst got his bonce stove in with a poker.'

'No, no . . . not that,' she cried, frowning heavily. 'Sammy has disappeared and we've simply got to find him.'

'Who's we?'

'Ed, you've got to help me.' She brought everything into play – glowing eyes, tossing curls, batting black-spider lashes and jutting provocative bosom. She had me whether I liked it or not.

'What do you want me to do?' I groaned.

'Find Sammy for me,' she pleaded. 'Just find him.'

I looked her in the eye and told her straight: 'That might be

17

easier said than done – especially if he don't want to get himself found.'

'Listen, Ed.' Her voice was insistent. 'There's a lot more to this than you may realize.'

'No, there isn't,' I said. 'There's always more to murder than first meets the eye – but I never make the mistake of not realizing it. That's why I never take on murder investigations.'

'Don't try to be facetious.' I subsided. 'I'm going to tell you the full strength of the situation.' I raised an eyebrow at her use of Cockney phraseology, but she brushed it, metaphorically speaking, aside.

'Sammy is in terrible danger. You thought that we hired you to watch Sonia and Patrick so as to get something on them and help Sammy with his divorce.'

'My speciality,' I put in modestly.

'Well, that wasn't really the reason at all. We had to know what they were doing – all the time. Tomlinson is a vile, low criminal. He was blackmailing Sammy.'

'Hold it right there,' I said. 'Why was he putting the black on Sir Samford?'

'I can't tell you that,' Pru muttered, tears in her eyes. She searched in her handbag for her handkerchief. Pinched her nose with it and turned her eyes on me. 'It was all to do with some wretched race horse. You know how mad Sammy is about horses. He lives for them. He was born to gamble – and win. You haven't been with him to a race meeting. If you had you'd know what I mean . . . He just wills his horse to come first past the winning post. It's the same with poker. His eyes literally smoulder and he will bet thousands and thousands on a single hand . . . even when he knows that he cannot win. . . .'

She was getting schmaltzy and I thought it was time to intervene.

'Sounds like a mug punter to me,' I said. 'What do you want me to do?'

She stared at me. I stared back.

'It was Tomlinson,' she said. 'I'm sure it must've been Tomlinson. He was blackmailing Sammy, as I said, really bleeding him white. And Parkhurst was devoted to Sammy. They'd been through the Korean war together and Parkhurst would

18

have done anything, really anything, to protect Sammy. He must've threatened Patrick, tried to stop him from bleeding Sammy, and Patrick killed him. I know Patrick murdered him. He would kill anyone who stood in his way.'

'Sounds a bit far-fetched to me,' I commented and lit a cigarette.

She reached into her handbag and drew out a bulging manilla envelope. My eyes blinked at the wad of fivers that peeped from the open flap.

'Go down to Bramley Hall and find out what's happening.' She tossed the envelope on my desk. 'I'm doubling your retainer and doubling your fee,' she purred. 'But you've got to find Sammy.'

I squeezed the envelope lightly between a forefinger and thumb. A weary smile and a helpless shrug were my thanks to her.

'How do you know I won't take your money and spend it on drink?' I asked.

She sighed extravagantly.

'I don't,' she said.

CHAPTER FOUR

Pru's two-and-a-half was a handy windfall. I paid the telephone bill and a month's back rent. I got my shirts out of the Chinese laundry round the corner and nipped over to Regent Street and kitted myself out with one of Austin Reed's trendy, off-the-peg, navy-blue two-piece worsteds, single-breasted – it looked like this case was going to be a dressy affair. I then purchased a couple of bottles of Hankey Bannister's and did a little solitary drinking in my office – it's a mug's game to pay for whisky in pubs by the nip when you can get it cheaper by the bottle from the off-licence. When I awoke next morning one bottle was empty. The smoke-grey light of dawn hung dismally over Piccadilly. It was early. I glanced at my watch – 7 o'clock. Too much whisky knocks you out all right, but the damage it does to your innards while you sleep wakes you up early.

I made a pot of tea and fell to thinking. What the hell was I doing getting myself mixed up in a murder case? It was against my principles to get dragged in on murder cases and I'd've been doing myself a not inconsiderable favour if I'd spent Pru's retainer on getting my head shrunk. Still, I told myself, all I've agreed to do is look for Sir Samford and that's all I'm going to do. If, as seemed more than probable, he turned out to be the murderer – I wasn't going to look for him all that hard. It was pretty woolly reasoning but the best I could do in the throes of a hangover.

Pru had suggested that I go down to Bramley Hall and see what was buzzing between Lady Sonia and her blackmailing swain. It seemed like a good idea and no less dangerous than sticking my head between the jaws of a tiger.

I fished out my road atlas of Great Britain from the bottom drawer of the desk and soon discovered that the village of Bramley lay sixty-four miles out of London down the A 30.

I lifted the telephone to see if it was working and, when it purred back at me, ruffled through the papers in my top drawer to find the number of Bramley Hall. People who live in swanky stately homes, with a lot of rooms and long corridors, have to run a long way to answer the phone. It rang for an interminable three minutes before Tomlinson came on the line.

'Who is it?'

'Ed Nelson.'

'Ed, who?'

'Nelson.'

'Are you a journalist?'

'No, I'm a private detective.'

'What do you want?'

'My principal has instructed me that Sir Samford must be found without delay. Your cooperation and that of Lady Sonia is of paramount importance, if I am to run him to ground before the police do. I shall be with you by eleven.' I hung up before he had time to give me an argument.

My rusty old Morris 1100 had more things wrong with her internal organs than a chain-smoking alcoholic geriatric. Her steering was faulty, her brakes sluggish. She leaked oil, her water boiled, her clutch slipped and she got winded on hills. She complained bitterly if I pushed her speedometer over fifty m.p.h. Once a year I frightened God with a sudden prayer that she'd somehow scrape through her Ministry of Transport roadworthiness test and against all the odds she always did. Maybe God heard my prayer. If not, it was on the cards that the miraculous recovery of her general mechanical condition on annual inspection day was due entirely to the five pound note with which I greased the examiner's palm.

I estimated that the drive to Bramley would take two hours. In the event it took three and a quarter. The slowness of our pace was in no way the fault of my faithful old roadster. It was simply that a force greater than my own willpower compelled me to pause for a sip of whisky in no less than three rose-covered taverns along the way. It is better to arrive late for an appointment, but in the peak of condition, than early with a hangover.

At the Silchester roundabout a signpost to Bramley took me off the main drag and for five or six miles I nosed my old banger along winding country lanes flanked by hedgerows ablaze with wild foxgloves, Solomon's seal, ragwort and stinging nettles. No sooner had I convinced myself that I was lost – feeling lost being a characteristic of city slickers the moment they clap eyes on a blade of grass – than a sign at the side of the road, partially obscured by ivy, said 'BRAMLEY. Please drive slowly through the village.'

The Peveril country seat was situated on the far side of the village. There was no mistaking the entrance. The local bobby stood sentinel outside the massive wrought-iron gates. The gates were supported by two brick pillars topped with granite pineapples, the symbol of hospitality.

I drew up beside the copper, wound down my window and popped my head out.

'Bramley Hall?' I asked.

He stepped up to the car and stooped a little to get a closer look at me. He had a ruddy complexion. His hair was greying at the temples and his eyes were as blue and crystal clear as a lagoon. The laughter lines around his eyes and at the corners of his mouth belied his stern expression. The quality of a man's life is reflected by such things.

He touched his helmet with a crooked finger as though tugging an invisible forelock.

'Be you a newspaper man, zur?' he enquired politely.

'Certainly not,' I retorted. 'I'm a private investigator from London.'

He looked unconvinced so I flashed my card under his nose. He looked at it and his lips moved as he read what was printed on it: 'ED NELSON, SURVEILLANCE EXPERT. DIVORCE. MISSING PERSONS. UNDERCOVER INVESTIGATIONS.'

'Hmmm,' he mused and produced a notebook and pencil from his breast pocket. 'Us've had a lot of people down from Lun'on since the murder, zur.' A smile lit up his face like a sunset. 'Us've already sent two television camera crews packing this morning.'

'I had an eleven o'clock appointment with Lady Sonia,' I said. 'Spoke to them on the phone this morning – I'm a bit late, I'm afraid.'

'I suppose it's all right for you to go in, zur. But us'll have to report your visit to the Inspector.' He scratched the back of his neck with his pencil. 'Us'll not book you for having worn tyres, zur. But it would be in your own best interests to get them changed.'

'Much obliged, officer,' I replied penitently and accelerated up the gravel drive.

Bramley Hall, when it loomed into view, was a Jacobean manor house built in the shape of a Roman H round about the time that Guy Fawkes tried to blow up the Houses of Parliament. Barley-sugar chimneys spiralled majestically from the roof and a dense growth of virginia creeper completely obliterated the facade. Off to one side loomed a number of bulky out-buildings which I presumed to be stables. There, no doubt, dwelt those four-footed beasts with whom Pru shared Sir Samford's affections.

The trim front lawn was dotted with topiary shrubs, clipped into birds. The family Rolls was parked in front of the porch. I lurched up behind it, cut the engine and clambered out of the car. A spritely lady came hurrying around the side of the house.

She had on a strange floppy-brimmed hat that partly obscured her vision and was carrying a garden cradle of flowers.

'Good afternoon,' I said as she came abreast of me.

'Good heavens!' she yelped and tore off in the direction from which she came, leaving a trail of flowers in her wake.

A private eye learns not to be surprised by such things.

I strode confidently up to the heavy front door, pressed the bell and waited. When no one came, I pressed it again, this time more urgently. Some moments later the door was opened by an elegant woman in a tweed skirt, twin-set and pearls.

'Lady Sonia Peveril?'

She gave me a welcoming smile.

'Mr Nelson, isn't it?'

'Yes, sorry I'm late . . .'

'. . . Not at all, not at all.' She waved my apology aside. 'It is I who should offer you the most fearful apologies for keeping you waiting on the doorstep. Do come in, do please come in. You're just in time for lunch.'

It was pretty far removed from the reception that I'd expected. It crossed my mind that she and Tomlinson had decided to lure me into the parlour and do me in.

I stepped over the threshold and offered her my hand. She touched it lightly and closed the front door. I followed her into a large dark hall hung with meticulously worked panels of moth-eaten tapestry and dominated by a massive richly carved staircase. At the foot of it lurked a tall, dark and handsome young man in an immaculately cut hound's tooth hacking jacket. It was Patrick Tomlinson. I recognized him instantly, as I had Lady Sonia the moment she opened the front door to me – I had after all been shadowing them for the past three weeks as they traipsed hand in hand around the night spots of Mayfair. Tomlinson had the kind of movie actor good looks that girls swoon over and men despise. Sonia was ten or fifteen years his senior, but in dazzling good nick.

'Patrick dear, this is Mr Nelson,' said Sonia. 'He's a private detective.'

He strolled over and we shook hands.

'We spoke on the phone,' he grunted and gave me the once over. People rarely take to me at first sight.

23

An ample woman in an apron came barging out of a door to the left of the stairs and said: 'Lunch will be ready in ten minutes, m'lady.'

'Thank you, Mrs Dixon,' said the lady of the house. 'Where's Mrs Davenport?'

'Haven't seen her since breakfast, mum,' Mrs Dixon came back at her crossly.

Lady Sonia sighed audibly.

'Do see if you can find her – she's probably in the greenhouse.'

Mrs Dixon bobbed an elephantine curtsy and departed grumbling.

'I think we could all do with a drink before lunch,' said Lady Sonia and led the way into a comfortable drawing-room.

'What will you have to drink, Mr Nelson?' asked Tomlinson.

'Scotch and soda,' I said. 'Hankey Bannister's if you have it.'

'You have me there, old boy.' He scanned the array of bottles on the Regency side table. 'I don't believe that is a brand I've ever heard of. Will Bell's do?'

'Fine.'

Lady Sonia fluttered an elegant hand in the direction of a chintz-covered armchair.

'Do sit down, Mr Nelson.'

I settled myself in the chair, took a gulp of whisky and gave her a fatuous smile.

'It's very kind of you to put up with me barging in on you like this. You must've had a terrible shock.'

Her mouth twisted and a nerve started twitching in her cheek.

'Oh, it's been awful. Quite awful,' she said very softly. 'Poor Parkhurst . . . and all those lovely diamonds . . .' she checked herself. 'Patrick tells me that you are looking for Samford. It is terribly dangerous, what you are doing. I don't know if you realize that.'

The thought had, of course, occurred to me but I didn't quite see what she was driving at. I grunted and raised an interrogative eyebrow.

'Samford is my husband and I know him terribly well.' She paused and did a bit of clenching and unclenching of her hands.

'What Sonia is trying to say,' cut in Tomlinson, 'is that we're very worried about Samford. I expect you've been briefed and

24

know already that he's badly dipped. His horses haven't been winning and we know that he has a big gambling debt outstanding that he cannot pay.'

'Gambling is second nature to him, of course,' she interrupted, 'but he's been so moody, violent and argumentative – I just know that something must be troubling him.'

'Only a few people know *exactly* what's troubling them,' I put in rather enigmatically.

Sonia and Patrick peeked at each other around the corner of their eyes.

'Annoying people seems to be the only pleasure he has left in life,' cried Sonia with unconcealed anger.

Tomlinson gave her an anxious look, then tossed me a watery smile.

'It's been frightfully upsetting,' he said. 'Sonia actually heard him . . . you tell him, darling.'

Sonia was gnawing at her lacquered nails. The skin was stretched over the aristocratic bone structure of her face and she seemed close to tears. I tried to work out why I wasn't feeling sorry for her and, for want of a better reason, put it down to the deep-seated mistrust the lower orders have of the wealthy.

'It seems like a terrible thing to say,' she murmured. There are several conventional preambles that a lady can choose from when she's about to bad-mouth her husband. 'It was only last week . . . What? Four or five days ago. I was going out to meet Patrick for dinner and I heard them shouting at each other in the library. It was Samford and Parkhurst and they were going for each other hammer and tongs. . . . I couldn't make out what they were saying . . . not the actual words. But they were screaming at each other. I heard a struggle and the furniture crashing about. I suppose it was awfully cowardly of me, but I just slipped out of the front door and hoped neither of them had heard me.'

'Not cowardly, darling, only sensible.'

'Parkhurst was Samford's batman in the war – the Korean war, you know. They went through a lot of terrifically heroic things together. Parkhurst has always been quite devoted to Samford, would do anything for him. But all the same he really was a most terrible moralist. He thoroughly disapproved of

25

Samford's way of life and felt that it was his duty to say so. Not to anyone else, of course, just to Samford. And with Samford in this strange overwrought, violent state. . . . Well, anything could have happened.'

I gazed at them blankly. I'd thought Pru had been a bit hopeful in thinking they might provide a clue to Samford's whereabouts. But it hadn't occurred to me that they'd be falling over each other to pin the murder on him.

They were looking at me now expectantly. It was clear that they were as nervous as alley cats.

I gave them a fleeting, rueful smile.

'I'm not investigating the murder, you know.'

A gloomy silence ensued. Before it got embarrassing Mrs Dixon stuck her head round the door.

'If you don't come and eat your lunch now this minute it'll be ruined,' she said and ducked out without waiting for a reply.

The tension relaxed a trifle.

'Mrs D. is such a poppet,' Tomlinson remarked. 'But she rules us all with a rod of iron.'

Lady Sonia got to her feet with an acrobat's grace and headed for the door with Tomlinson in hot pursuit. I quaffed my drink and brought up the rear with a fag dangling out of the side of my mouth.

The atmosphere as we sat down to lunch, in the pine-panelled dining room, was rather reserved. But things livened up a bit when Mrs Davenport, the lady I'd startled upon my arrival, came bustling in half-way through the first course. The absence of her hat revealed a thin weather-beaten face, sparkling humorous eyes and a thatch of silver hair cut into an Eton crop. She was quite short, not much over five feet, and in her late fifties. She looked like a nice little soul, but somehow the Mrs didn't suit her. I wondered where she got it from.

'Cousin Elinor, you're late again,' scolded Lady Sonia.

'I'm so sorry,' said Elinor. 'An absolutely too perfectly sweet little mistle thrush is nesting in the orchard and I lost all track of time watching her settle in.'

Lady Sonia's voice was unnecessarily cross.

'What on earth are we to do with you!'

'I think it's very delightful of a dear little mistle thrush to want

26

to come and live with us,' Elinor's eyes alighted on me. 'Don't you agree Mr . . . er?'

I lurched to my feet.

'Nelson – Ed Nelson.'

She held out a thin sunburned hand and gave me a warm friendly smile.

'I think it's just fine,' I said as we shook hands. 'I only wish a mistle thrush would come and live on my window ledge – all I've got is Cockney pigeons.'

'Good gracious,' cried Elinor and began spooning soup into her mouth as though a famine was imminent.

Lady Sonia tut-tutted disapprovingly.

Elinor looked up sheepishly, shrugged and continued spooning even more gluttonously than before. I found myself liking her.

'It must be nice living in the country,' I said when eventually her spoon came to rest. 'Close to nature and all that . . .?'

A little small talk seemed like a good way of relieving the tense silence that had again descended.

'I adore the country, of course,' Elinor said. 'But I always look forward to my occasional visits to London tremendously – all those glittering lights and wonderful theatres are perfectly thrilling. Do you like the theatre?'

'Never find time to go.'

'I think I like musicals best. Now what was the delightful show Sammy took me to a few months ago? It's on at the what's-it-called, that lovely theatre on the corner of Charing Cross Road, what *was* it called? Good heavens, my memory! It's got that dreadful what's-her-name in it. She was in that marvellous play with darling Sir Thingummy, with the splendid speaking voice, last year. Anyway she was certainly in it, but she was frightfully mis-cast. What was it called? Oh dear, I'll forget my own name next.'

Lady Sonia tinkled a small silver hand bell and Mrs Dixon came thundering in with a dish of cold meat and a bowl of salad.

'When did you last see Sir Samford?' I asked Elinor as we tucked into the cold collation.

She was so preoccupied with shovelling food into her mouth that she didn't hear my question. I repeated it.

27

'Last weekend, I think.' Elinor glanced at the other two for confirmation. 'It was last weekend, wasn't it?'

Patrick Tomlinson cleared his throat and lowered his fork. He seemed to be making a decision. I wondered if it was whether or not he should throw me bodily out of the house. Lady Sonia was gazing at him with an agonized look on her face. I had a feeling that it was an expression I'd come to know well if my investigation of this case went on for long. 'We saw him last night.'

The effect of the announcement was precise, sharp and alarming. Elinor choked, Sonia started trembling, I knocked my glass over and a fast-moving stream of claret flowed across the highly polished table and cascaded like a waterfall into Patrick's lap.

I started mopping up the spilt wine with my white damask table napkin.

It was definitely Patrick's turn to spill the beans. He ignored his soggy crotch and got on with it.

'It was very late. Sonia and I were just having a night cap before turning in. There was a crunch of feet on the gravel outside the french windows. And the next thing we knew Samford was in the room, dishevelled, with a mad light in his eyes. He hardly seemed to know what he was doing, or even where he was, but he snapped at us to keep quiet – and never to tell a soul that we'd seen him. Then he dashed out of the room and we heard him going upstairs, two at a time. We were frightened. I have to say it, we were absolutely petrified, and huddled over the fire waiting to see what would happen next.

'We could hear him banging about upstairs and ten minutes or so later, he burst back into the room. This time he was carrying a large suitcase. His eyes were completely insane and he glared at us wildly. He said: "You'll never see me again – this is it." And went out the way he'd come.'

'Nonsense,' said Elinor, who'd now got her jaws back under control. I was inclined to agree with her. 'I'm a light sleeper, the slightest sound wakes me up. But I never heard a thing,' she added and tucked another helping of meat and mixed salad into her mouth.

'It's true. It's true,' yelped Sonia and turned on me with a look of passionate appeal. 'Should we tell the police about it?'

I decided to be of no comfort to anyone.

'Suit yourselves,' I replied.

I spurned the offer of coffee and made my escape. I didn't think I could hang around any longer without doing my nut. As the old banger coughed and wheezed its way down the drive, I experienced an overwhelming sense of relief.

When I reached the gate into the road, there was no sign of the country bobby. His place had apparently been taken by a little rat of a man with a large felt hat pulled down over his eyes. Half a mile further on, as I coasted downhill towards the village, I passed a big geezer with a rotten face and massive shoulders sitting in the hedge lighting a torpedo cigar.

CHAPTER FIVE

Although I was reasonably certain that Sir Samford had not been kidnapped by a gang of ruthless jewel thieves, I'd not ruled out the possibility that an underworld cracksman had deftly screwed the peter and lifted the family sparklers. It was, with a good stretch of the imagination, just conceivable that the theft of the tom was not directly linked to the murder, or the Baronet's disappearance – wild reasoning, I'll admit, especially when the most obvious solution was that Sir Samford had, for reasons best known to himself, bumped off his own butler and made off with his own gems for parts unknown. This, as the headlines of the London evening papers testified, was the level-headed opinion of Superintendent Clews.

I ditched my wheezing old banger on my favourite out-of-order parking meter in St James's and pinched a copy of the *Evening Standard* from the we-trust-you newspaper stand on the corner of Duke Street. I scanned the story as I made my way back to the office.

There were banner SHOCK, HORROR, SENSATION headlines that left one in no doubt that Sir Samford had gone off his rocker and filled in his butler. Though they hedged a bit, here and there, on account of libel possibilities.

The *Standard* is a linen that gets news on the street fast.

Sonia and Tomlinson appeared to have been busy on the blower after I left. They'd passed on their extraordinary story about Samford busting into Bramley Hall at the dead of night in direct quotes, and the newsmen had swallowed the scoop whole.

The police request for information on the Baronet's present whereabouts, which had appeared in the previous day's paper, had paid dividends in no uncertain manner. It is, after all, only human for citizens to take a keen interest in their neighbour's business and grass them to the law whenever possible. He'd been spotted in Brussels, Cardiff, Leighton Buzzard, Land's End and Croydon. The police had so far failed to have a word with him.

The juicy story finished up with the news that police were keeping a sharp eye on London Airport and the Channel ferries. Fair enough as far as it went. The authorities always keep a watch for fugitives on legitimate points of departure from the country and, unless the hunted man is round the twist, they always come up empty-handed.

That night, armed with the confidence that city slickers derive from the feel of a solid pavement beneath their feet, I ventured furtively through the murky byways of Soho – that square mile of London vice where, if the gutter press are to be believed, every narrow, twisting alley is infested with junkie muggers and a man's shadow is seldom his own.

It'd crossed my mind that if Pru was reading the linens she would, as usual, be pretty ratty. Everything that I'd discovered at Bramley was already common knowledge. If I was to avoid the sticky moment when she'd start demanding her two-and-a-half back, I'd better come up with some information of a confidential nature and be pretty damn quick about it. The underworld knows everything there is to know about hot items of value so I decided to try and pick up a whisper on the fate of the Peveril gems.

I threaded my way down the rows of strip-joints, knocking shops and dens of iniquity, and fetched up at last outside a sleazy basement shpieler in Berwick Street called the Hide Away Club. I jammed a cigarette into the corner of my mouth and entered looking tough.

'Wotcha, Ed,' rasped the minder on the door. 'Doin' any good?'

'Not so's you'd notice,' I sneered at him. 'Diamonds Silverman been down t'night?'

Len Stokes was a professional minder, minder being common parlance in the underworld for a bodyguard. Now in his middle fifties, he had been minding people for the whole of his adult life, and rumour had it, he first offered his minding talents to his school mates when he was ten or eleven and charged them a tanner a week for services rendered. Those silly enough to turn him down usually had their minds changed by the time he had finished giving them a free demonstration of what he had on offer. Shattered knee-caps and the expert use of a blade were optional extras. This early apprenticeship had served him in good stead, and by the age of forty he had minded some of the biggest tearaways in the British Isles: French Herbert, One-Eared Jock, Tony Pappegeottes, Lime-House Lorrie, the list was endless. Len was a bad-faced, heavy-fisted pug and he'd made a good living out of punching transgressors into the middle of next week. He'd gone to gut, but he wasn't past it, and was now minding Willy Paradis, the proprietor of the Hide Away. The gang wars now being long over, gambling no longer illegal and Soho's prostitutes having gone to ground, life for Len had become extremely peaceful. No one but the occasional rowdy football fan needed chinning any longer, and his function as a minder was little more than window dressing.

A cunning glint came into Len's eyes and his battered old face twisted into a humourless smile.

'Yuh got some bent tom yuh wanna flog?'

I glanced furtively about and whispered in his ear.

'I just knocked off the crown jewels.'

He let out a guttural laugh and thumped me firmly between the shoulder blades.

'I reckon Diamonds Silverman is the only fence on the manor wiv the right kinda connections in Amsterdam to get that lot busted up an' got back on the market as free fousand engagement rings,' he said.

'Have you seen him?'

''E ain't put in an appearance yet, but 'e shows up most nights, sure as eggs is eggs.'

'Any particular time?'

31

' 'E's gone off his rocker over a stripper called Gloria Randy,' chuckled Len. 'She drops 'er drawers somethin' rotten at the Glass Slipper till midnight, then comes 'ere for a couple a drinks an' drives old Diamonds round the bend wiv false promises. 'E usually shows up about half eleven an' waits for 'er wiv 'is tongue 'angin' out.'

'Sounds like he's got it bad.'

Len raised his hands, palms towards the heavens, and shrugged his massive shoulders.

'Fat lotta good it'll do 'im – that Gloria's a right prick teaser. She'll con 'im somethin' rotten, then give 'im the elbow soon as 'e gets naughty about not gettin' into her knickers.'

I glanced at my watch. It was ten forty-five. 'Mind if I hang about 'til he shows up?'

'Suitcha self, Ed,' said Len. 'But no askin' the punters dodgy questions about any villainy that's come off lately – I know you ain't never grassed no one in yuh life, but some of the 'ounds don't know that an' they're liable to turn stroppy, know what I mean?'

I snorted and made my way to the bar.

The Hide Away was, to the criminal classes, what the United Universities club is to academics – a place where graduates socialize. In the same way that a university graduate with a double first is likely to command greater respect than lesser mortals with second or third class degrees, the bank robber and the jewel thief are the princes of the underworld while the shoplifter and common burglar are mere serfs. If all the time that all the members of the Hide Away had served behind bars was added together it would stretch back to the Crucifixion – the more years an old lag had put in at the bad boys' academy, the greater the esteem in which he was held amongst this lawless fraternity.

In its own uncompromising way the Hide Away was as exclusive as the Ritz and, given the transient nature of ill-gotten gains, the clientele was often as rich. It had a kind of sleazy opulence that was both alluring and frightening — the atmosphere in which villains feel at home and honest, law-abiding folk are decidedly ill at ease.

The bar was lined with dark-suited tearaways, sipping good old whisky in the company of bad young girls. A poker school was in progress in a dark corner. In the centre of the room a roulette wheel was spinning merrily and, behind a boomerang shaped table against the wall, a dark-skinned girl in a chalky blonde wig was

32

dealing marked cards to black-jack enthusiasts.

Willy Paradis was perched on his usual stool at the corner of the bar. He was a thin evil-faced man in his late fifties. He was got up in immaculate, gangsters' uniform, identical to the men around him − dark suit with heavily padded shoulders, snow-white shirt and conservative tie. He looked tired.

He glanced around as I approached. His eyes were wary but not hostile.

' 'Ello, loser,' He called everybody 'loser' except maybe his mother. 'Wotcha drinkin'?'

'Hankey Bannister's.'

' 'Ankey Bannister's,' he said to the pug behind the bar. 'Make it a large one.'

'How's business?' I asked.

He made a see-saw motion with his left hand. A solitaire diamond the size of a golf ball sparkled on his pinky.

'Up and down like Tower Bridge,' he grunted. ' 'Ow's it wiv you?'

I shrugged.

'Nothing changes but the date.'

The barman brought my drink. I toasted Willy and drank mightily.

'On a case?' he asked menacingly. A life-time of talking like a movie gangster had rendered him incapable of passing the time of day without making it sound like a threat.

I said, 'You could say so.'

'Who's yuh client?'

Unlike the police it is safer to tell gangsters the truth.

'I'm sort of working on the dead butler caper,' I said. 'You've read the headlines?'

'Yeah, some nob in Belgravia 'as bin bumpin' orf the 'elp?'

'Looks that way.'

Willy laughed heartily and slapped his thigh.

'Bin doin' the same fing meself for years,' he declared. 'Not so much now as in the old days. But it always was best to get rid of geezers wot knew enough to put the finger on yuh − it's wot they call redundant nowerdays, ain't it?'

I polished off the remains of my drink and a refill appeared as if by magic. I glanced along the bar and caught sight of Big

Ronnie, an East End razor king who inadvertently owed me a favour. I had done a fair number of favours for various members of the underworld over the years, mainly by keeping my trap shut about crimes the CID would dearly like to solve.

'Don't shit on your own door-step', is the first rule in the private eye's handbook.

I nodded my thanks for the drink to Big Ronnie and returned my attention to Willy.

'' 'Obnobbin' with the upper crust ain't exactly your usual game, Ed?' he said.

'Only when I get lucky.'

''Ow did yuh get on the case?'

'By accident.'

'Uh?'

'I was doing a bit of straight forward divorce snooping for some chick when all of a sudden her high-born lover does a disappearing act and she bungs me a few quid to find him for her.'

'Who is 'e?'

'Same bloke the law are after – Sir Samford Peveril.'

Something akin to amusement lit up Willy's face.

'Well yuh ain't likely to find 'im down 'ere, are yuh?'

'I didn't expect to.' I smiled. 'But the family jewels have gone on the missing list and I thought it might be worth asking Diamonds Silverman if any of it has come his way – in the strictest confidence, of course.'

'Diamonds is certainly a character who knows a lot about 'ot tomfoolery,' said Willy. 'But 'e ain't 'ad 'is mind on 'is work lately. . .'

'Len told me he's got it bad over Gloria Randy.'

Willy eyed me speculatively.

'That's as maybe,' he said. 'But there's more to it than wotcha might fink.'

'Like what?'

The corners of his mouth twisted into a smile.

'Bein' as 'ow you're a mate I don't reckon it'll do all that much 'arm if I mark yuh card.'

Willy wasn't the kind of bloke who went around doing people favours.

'Much obliged,' I replied guardedly.

34

'Yuh know that upper class bloke yuh mention – wot filled in his butler?'

'Sir Samford Peveril?'

'That's the fella. Well, the butler was no one else but Gloria's older bruvva.'

My face slumped.

'Do me a favour, Willy. Pull the other one, it's got bells on.'

A wounded expression passed over his face.

'Straight up,' he assured me. 'Gloria was 'is skin and blister and 'e was a right no good sod, if wot I 'ear about 'im is anyfing to go by, which most times it ain't.'

I gazed at him in disbelief for a moment or two, then gulped my whisky – it went down the wrong hole and I nearly choked to death. Willy thumped me heavily on the back until I'd recovered and said: 'Just watcha step, mate, if yuh finkin' of stickin' yuh hooter in that little love nest.'

If Gloria Randy really was Parkhurst's sister, it was definitely on the cards that Willy had some highly dodgy reason for sharing the information with me. It probably meant that he was involved in some way – I wondered if I ought to ask him if he was acquainted with any of the tearaways I'd seen holding up lamp-posts around the manor but decided that it might be the kind of question that he would get cross about.

As if on cue a tall tarty girl breezed into the joint and, glancing to left and right, made her way to the bar. As she drew closer I saw that she had blotchy skin, big boobs and spaces between her teeth. She was no oil painting, but sexy in a sensual sort of way. The hounds made room for her at the bar and Willy said:

'Diamonds ain't bin down yet, Gloria.'

'He'll show,' she replied confidently and gave me the once over.

I didn't really recognize her, but being a frequenter of cellar strip joints, I'd probably seen her doffing her clobber once or twice.

'Gloria,' said Willy, 'this is Ed, 'e's okay.'

He knew better than tell her my line of work, or that I too was waiting for Diamonds. Girls can get very nosey.

She gave me a glassy stare; her eye lids were puffy and inflamed as though she'd been crying a lot recently.

35

CHAPTER SIX

It was well past midnight when Diamonds Silverman eventually put in an appearance. He was a tub of lard rounded into an over-strained pin-striped business suit. Plugged into the corner of his mouth was the butt of an evil-smelling cigar and his sagging jowls were fixed in a permanent scowl. He was as Jewish as *schmalz-herring* and cunning like a fox.

'Where've you been?' Gloria petulantly demanded as he waddled to her side. 'You promised to take me to the Marabu.'

He fixed her with sad eyes and answered with an ill-tempered Yiddish bull-frog in his throat.

'Yuh don't know vot ah tavour yuh do by me, Gloria, if yuh leave off from unkindness to me in public. It don't look good.'

Gloria tucked her lower lip behind her teeth.

'I've got a lot better things to do than hang about in low dives waiting for you to show up in your own sweet time.'

Diamonds placed an affectionate meaty paw on her arm.

'Yuh makin' me a headache,' he said and beckoned to the barman. 'Anisette, double anisette.' He hooked me with his eyes and attempted a smile. 'Look, am I a nice man?'

'Shure, mishter Shilverman,' I slurred. 'One of the besht . . .'

I'd been on the premises for more than two hours and was three-quarters sloshed on free whisky. The drinks had come thick and fast and, such is the lavish generosity of vagabonds and thieves when their pockets are lined, I'd not been permitted to pay for a single round.

Before Diamonds showed up I'd plugged into Gloria's conversation in the hope of picking up a tit-bit or two. But far from sobbing out in graphic detail the inside story of her brother's demise, Gloria had whiled away the time in bawdy repartee with a group of punters who clearly fancied her. Their chat was pretty tedious so I just kept swamping back the booze.

Diamonds jerked a podgy thumb in Gloria's direction.

'Such a bootiful girl! Don't I give 'er everything 'er 'eart desires? But vot does she give me in return? Nutting but aggravation, dat's vot.' He couldn't't've looked more depressed if he'd just shoved his mother off a bridge. 'She does me no tavours. Jewels an' furs I give 'er, but not even a little tavour.'

'Whatever turns you on,' I quipped.

Gloria held out a slender jewel-encrusted hand for my inspection and let out a scornful little laugh.

'I've got the hottest fingers in town,' she said contemptuously. 'One of these days I'm gonna get my collar felt for receiving.'

Diamonds' professional reputation had been slighted; he was deeply wounded. He cursed in Hebrew.

'Yemach shemo ve'zichro! Ven Silverman cut a bent rock no one recognize it ever again. Not de cops an', my life, not even de biggest expert in 'Atton Garden!'

The clientele of the Hide Away, who'd lent half an ear to the conversation, nodded their profound agreement. None would've denied that Diamonds was the greatest cutter and re-setter of hot tom in the world. But it was unwise to boast of such things in public and Willy Paradis told the gross old fence to keep his voice down.

Later, when he'd drunk off six glasses of anisette and his frame of mind had slightly improved, I took him aside and casually mentioned that I had an interest in the gems that'd gone missing from the Peveril's swank residence in Belgravia. I was careful not to mention anything about Gloria.

Diamonds' reaction was predictably guarded.

'Vot for yuh arst me? I don't know nutting about nutting.'

His toad-like face turned a fiery red colour and he started panting as if he was short of breath. My tie fluttered in the breeze and, sloshed though I was, I found it unnerving.

I got together the most reassuring tone of voice I could.

'Jusht ashkin', jusht ashkin'.'

'I don't know nutting,' he repeated with a snort.

'Jusht putting you in the know,' I explained. 'Any little whisper you could put my way . . . Might be a nishe few quid in it.' I whined winsomely and added, 'Big reward going, I'd shay . . . matter of thoushands. If that'sh of any interesht to you.' I was romancing of course, but I couldn't see Diamonds giving me the time of day unless there was a few quid in it.

His heightened colour ebbed away, and he stroked his triple chin with a finger and thumb.

Now and then, when an insurance company showed the good sense to offer a substantial reward for the return of certain high quality merchandise – no questions asked – the missing goods made a miraculous reappearance. Diamonds himself had never actually been the official recipient of such a reward. But there never had been, and never was likely to be, a gem adrift in the underworld whose whereabouts he was not aware of. It was tacitly accepted, by all parties concerned, that Diamonds must certainly have had a hand in any deal that eventually led to a dowager being reunited with her tiara or a tearful housewife with her engagement ring.

'Vot offer yuh tink dey make?'

I shrugged my shoulders.

'Dunno,' I admitted.' But from all I hear, it'sh big . . . very, very big!'

'Like I already tell yuh I know nutting. But maybe, on de grapevine, I 'ear of somebody vants to return a few stones to deir rightful owner. If I do, I let yuh know.'

'You'll give me a ring?'

'Mit pleasure.'

I knew that this was the best I was going to do.

'Want a drink?'

'Anisette,' he said and rolled the short distance to Gloria's side.

'I wonna go to the Marabu,' she rasped. 'And I wonna go now.'

'Vimin,' moaned Diamonds. 'All dey do is vant dis and vant dat. Ven, I ask, do I get some return on de outlay?'

The fire-engine-red telephone on the corner of the bar jangled like a burglar alarm going off. Willy Paradis snatched up the receiver and put it to his ear.

'Right,' he snapped. 'Okay – five minutes – gotcha!' He slammed down the phone and hollered: 'Clews is on 'is way. Everybody oooooout!'

In two shakes of a lamb's tail the room was as deserted as Oxford Street on Christmas Day. Hard-drinking tearaways left rounds of drinks untouched on the bar and inveterate gamblers made a rapid departure without bothering to cash in their chips.

The five twenty-pound notes with which Willy straightened sergeant Sid Bradley every month insured that the Hide Away's early warning system never broke down. Sid had a responsible job in the operations room at the Yard. His wife had a mink coat, his only daughter roared around in a flashy sports car and buried in the cabbage patch of their sweet, little, rose-covered family holiday cottage in North Devon was a pouch full of Kruger rands. Or so it was widely rumoured in underworld circles. And it might well have been true for all I know.

Although I had nothing more than usual to hide, I had no wish to come face to chest with the lofty Super in a den of iniquity like the Hide Away.

At the corner of the street I lurked in the shadow of a darkened office building and watched Clews go sirening by in the back seat of a black police Wolseley. The car screeched to a halt outside Willy Paradis' establishment and the Superintendent got out clutching the crown of his head. Considering how often his skull came into smart contact with car roofs and door jambs it was surprising that his brains weren't scrambled.

I wonder whether Clews, with easy access to public records and police files, had rumbled Gloria Randy's connection with Parkhurst. Things didn't look too clever for Diamonds either and that might've brought him around here on the hurry-up. Not being bogged down with the police procedure of having to obtain a magistrate's warrant before I could pass through portals of sleazy dives, I'd got to the Hide Away ahead of the Super. However, there were still a few hours before sunrise. If he got lucky he might catch up with Diamonds at the Marabu.

The appearance of the law on the 'manor' made me nervous and I headed for home. Leaning bare-legged against a parked car in the Haymarket was Black Satin Hotpants. She smiled at me as I approached. With turgid tits, moist lips and wiggly bottom, she had dirty sex written all over her.

'Short time, darling?' she enquired brightly.

'How much?'

'Ten pounds for half-an-hour.'

'Make it five.'

'Okay.'

'Come on then.'

'Where to?'

I pointed across the road.

'I live over there in Regent Chambers.'

She trotted along beside me and made small talk.

'The law are all over the place like flies tonight,' she said. 'Nearly got busted three times.'

I made no reply.

'You're out late, where've you been?'

'Having dinner with the Queen.'

We'd reached my front door, I fumbled the latchkey into the lock and we went inside. My throat was dry and I already had a hard-on for her. As we travelled up to the third floor in the lift she leaned against the wood panelling with her legs slightly apart and gazed unabashed at the bulge straining the material of my trousers.

She flopped onto the horsehair sofa in my office and said: 'How do you want it – straight or French?'

I looked down at her. Her face was as immobile as a dinner plate.

'Half and half,' I said.

She hurried me off in five minutes flat, then left.

CHAPTER SEVEN

At noon the phone rang. It was Pru.

'Ed!' she shrilled. 'I've just seen Sammy.'

'Where?'

'In Bond Street,' she continued breathlessly. 'Something terrible must have happened – he ran away from me.'

'His butler has been savagely murdered. I expect it's preying on his mind.'

Static interference came on the line: a click, click, click and a buzz as though someone was getting a crossed line. Pru was saying something but it sounded as though she was phoning from Alaska in the middle of a blizzard.

Then a rasping cockney voice was on the line saying:

'Yuh've stuck the soddin' fing in the wrong 'ole, yuh burk! Can'tcha do nuffink right?'

'Leave off 'avin' a go at me – I'm doin' me best, ain't I,' a second voice snarled.

Then the blizzard started up again. There was a high pitched whine, a few more clicks, and Pru came through again. The desperation in her voice indicated that the part of our conversation I hadn't picked up had been pretty upsetting for her.

'. . . and there were shoppers and traffic but I dashed after him, calling out to him at the top of my voice . . . Oh Ed, you can't imagine what it was like – the faster I ran the further away he seemed to get and I nearly got run over several times. Then I thought I saw him go into Asprey's and I kept running until I got there. I pushed through the door like a wild thing and half a dozen of those men in morning coats and striped trousers descended on me. But they hadn't seen him. Nobody'd been in. I simply couldn't believe it, even when they let me search the place from top to bottom and he was nowhere to be found.'

Her voice petered out into a sob.

'I take it that you are referring to Sir Samford?'

'Of course, I am,' she wailed. 'Haven't I just been telling you?'

'There was a bit of interference on the line. I didn't catch all of it. Perhaps you could start again.'

She'd spotted the missing baronet in Bond Street. When she hailed him from the opposite side of the road he'd had it away on his toes a bit lively and disappeared off the face of the earth, or at least in a crowd of shoppers, and she'd be eternally grateful if I'd get stuck into running him to ground.

'I'll do my best,' I assured her. 'But he could be anywhere by now. . . . If, for example, he took a cab to Heathrow, he might be having lunch in Paris or Manchester.'

She let out an angry snort.

I began to tell her about my visit to Bramley Hall.

'Do you know any more than what I've already read in the papers?' she enquired contemptuously.

'No.'

'In that case, don't waste your breath and my time.'

After a bit of an argument about who was who's client and who was getting paid to find whom I eventually calmed her down and promised, rather lamely, to move heaven and earth in my effort to track down her boy friend.

41

'Why don't you go around to the Peveril place in Belgravia and see if he's been there?' she suggested.

'Good idea,' I said and it was. Though at the time I was only playing her along.

The phone clicked and buzzed as Pru hung up. I held the receiver to my ear for a moment or two to see if our cockney friends were still on the line.

'That it?' someone said.

'Pull the soddin' plug out, yuh burk,' said the second voice and the line went dead.

'Amateurs,' I sighed and cradled the receiver.

As I had expected Clews still had the Peveril gaff under surveillance, but the cherubic-looking constable who stood sentinel on the front doorstep was no deterrent and I gained access to the premises with ease, through a rear window.

There was no sign of Mrs Brown, the housekeeper, and I concluded – just as I'd hoped – that she was still recovering from shock at her sister-in-law's. Not surprisingly, there was also no sign of Sammy.

The afternoon sun filtered through the net curtains in the drawing room. There was ample light to make a thorough search and the curtains afforded a certain amount of privacy from the inquisitive glances of passers-by. But what the hell I was looking for was anybody's guess.

I rummaged about in the drawing room and came up with nothing of any interest. Then I went upstairs and turned the bedroom over. Again I came up empty handed. But in the attic I made a little progress.

Parkhurst's eyrie under the eaves of the house was instantly recognizable. The small bare room reflected the character of the meticulous man who had lived in it as indelibly as a tattoo on a sailor's arm. There was a neatness to the layout of the dead butler's effects that betrayed the orderly habits instilled by a lifetime of service. His hairbrushes and comb were laid out on top of the small chest of drawers as fastidiously as silver cutlery on a dining table. The blankets on the single bed against the wall were tucked in so tightly you could bounce a coin off them. The olive green linoleum floor-covering was as burnished as a field-marshal's Sam Browne, and his few clothes hung stiffly in the wardrobe as though an inspection was imminent. The overall effect was as spartan and uncomforting as a prison cell.

On a small table beneath the window was a framed photograph of an army sergeant with two rows of medal ribbons on his chest and a Coldstream Guards badge on his peaked cap. I returned my attention to the wardrobe and made a more thorough inspection of its contents. There were a couple of butler's monkey suits, a tweed sports jacket and flannels, and a dark lounge suit that he had probably worn to weddings and funerals. But there was no sign of the military uniform that he was wearing with such obvious pride in the photograph. Old sweats never part with their uniform until their dying day. Indeed, they will as likely as not, use up their last gasp with a request to be buried in it.

I sat down on the edge of the narrow bed and pondered on the matter for a time. It was the nearest I had come to a clue, but I regretfully decided that he must've packed the uniform away in moth-balls. Then I stole downstairs and went into the library. The books that had been scattered around the floor on my previous visit had been returned to their shelves – the murder room team had probably collected them up so that the forensic boys could examine the floor boards for traces of blood.

I slumped into a leather armchair, lit a cigarette and surveyed the room. The musty tomes that lined the walls looked as heavy going as a Labour party manifesto and, as if to scare off 'Philistines', plaster busts of Plato, Socrates, Byron, Shelley and Shakespeare looked down from plinths erected at regular intervals around the tops of the mahogany bookcases.

Puffing smoke into the air, my eye wandered from one to another of them absentmindedly and then, suddenly, I noticed that Shelley was looking in an ever so slightly different direction to his companions. My first thought was that the builder who put him up there must have been cross-eyed and my second was that someone had climbed up and moved it – why would anyone want to do that?

I got up out of the chair, dragged the library steps to the bookcase over which Shelley presided, and scrambled up for a closer look. He'd been moved all right, and recently at that – there were finger marks in the dust at the base of the bust where it rested on the plinth, and an eighth of an inch half circle of white marble was exposed where the bust had been replaced or moved into the wrong position. I cupped my hands about the head and was surprised by how easily I was able to lift it. I turned it over and discovered that the inside was hollow. Attached to one side with sellotape was a black velvet bag. I reached inside and wrenched it out. Its diamond-hard contents jabbed into my fingers. I quickly replaced Shelley on his plinth and half fell and half clambered to the floor.

The overpowering urge to get the hell out of there subdued my desire to inspect my lucky find there and then. I had a pretty good idea what would meet my eyes if I peeked into the bag. But I wasn't altogether sure that I'd be able to prevent myself from shouting: 'Eureka!' and by so doing attract the attention of the young bobby outside. Alternatively I might've thrown a scare into the two rotten-faced tearaways tinkering with a motorbike three lamp posts down.

CHAPTER EIGHT

Whoever it was that had used the bust of Shelley as a hiding place, for whatever it was that was burning a hole in my pocket, would be more than a little peeved when they tumbled that they'd gone missing. So, to make my trail just that much more difficult to follow, I returned to the West End by bus. A cab driver will snitch on his own mother for tuppence.

It wasn't until I'd securely locked myself behind my own door, jammed a chair under the handle for good measure, drawn the blinds and swigged a couple of hefty belts of Hankey Bannister's from the neck of the bottle, that I was ready to take a gander at the contents of the black velvet bag. Considering that I devoted most of my waking hours to poking my nose into other people's business, it was a wonder that I'd put it off for so long.

I sat down behind the desk, loosened the silk tape at the opening of the bag and spilled the tomfoolery onto the ink blotter. Such glitter! I blinked in disbelief. There before me was an array of sparklers that would've put Van Cleef and Arpels Paris window display in the shade. Fortified by a few more swigs of Hankey Bannister's I examined the collection more closely.

There was a pearl necklace, four strands of whoppers, with a diamond clasp shaped like a butterfly, a ring with a diamond as big as the Ritz in a ribbon of small emeralds, a sapphire and diamond tiara that came to bits with a pair of eardrops to match, six assorted brooches, all set with precious stones and a signet ring set with another dirty great emerald engraved with the Peveril stags. But the prize of the collection was an unbelievable triple-row necklace of graduated oval sapphires alternating with diamonds and rubies the size of quails' eggs. The whole lot was set in enough gold to fill the teeth of the entire congregation of Golders Green Synagogue.

Property, in the eyes of the law, being more precious than human life, I was inadvertently in possession of enough hot merchandise to get me twenty-five years in the slammer. I lit a cigarette, sipped a little more whisky, and pondered.

I could turn the gems over to Clews and maybe collect the insurance company reward. I could try to discover who put them in the bust of Shelley and why. I could hand them over to Lady Sonia or, most attractive of all, I could book a one-way passage on a tramp steamer to Venezuela and live out the rest of my days in the lap of luxury.

A light tap on the door interrupted my deliberations.

'Who's there?' I asked, alarmed.

'Ed!' It was a female voice and the door handle rattled.

'Let me in, I've got to talk to you.'

'Hold on a sec.'

I jerked open the top drawer of the desk and swept the jewels out of sight.

The knocking came again, this time more urgently.

'It's me, Pru – Prudence Pride. Please open the door.'

I locked the desk, gave the drawer a little tug to make sure it was secure, then crossed the room and let her in. In she breezed in a cloud of expensive scent, and threw herself down on the horse-hair sofa. She was wearing a flowered silk dress and Gucci shoes.

I wondered what her reaction would have been if I told her

she was sitting on the very spot where I'd made it with Black Satin Hotpants the night before.

For several moments she just sat there, trembling all over, and I just sat there looking at her.

'Why have you got the blinds drawn?' she stammered finally.

I leaned back in my chair, reached towards the window and drew them back.

'That better?'

The beam of sunlight that filtered through the Hankey Bannister's hoarding galvanized her into action. She began rummaging in her snake-skin handbag and spilt enough bottles and boxes of pills out onto the sofa to tranquillize a herd of stampeding elephants.

'Could I have a glass of water?' she asked. 'I'm having a nervous breakdown.'

I filled a plastic cup at the wash basin and handed it to her.

With shaking fingers she daintily selected a dozen or so multi-coloured uppers and downers and arranged them in a neat row on top of her handbag. They ranged from valium through vitamin pills to aspirin.

Like a bird pecking crumbs from a window-sill she popped one after another of them into her mouth and between each took a tiny sip of water from the plastic cup. When the last one had gurgled down her gullet, she set the cup down on the desk and pouted her lips to control an involuntary burp.

'I expect you feel a lot better now,' I said.

She turned her lustrous eyes on me and said:

'Well, have you found Sammy?'

' 'Fraid not.'

She let her lids close over her eyes for a moment. Then she peeked at me through her long mascara-ed lashes.

'Ed,' she murmured, 'do you think he could have done it?'

'Let me put it this way,' I said. 'He might have, on the one hand, and he might not have, on the other. The papers definitely think he did it, which probably means that the police do too. But that doesn't mean that either of them is right.'

'He ran away from me,' she said, 'actually ran away from me. I just can't get it out of my mind. It's driving me mad. . . . I

know that Sammy could never do anything as terrible as murder
... and yet ...' Her voice trailed away.

I pushed the pill bottles towards her.

'Have a few more,' I suggested. She fumbled a couple of
purple hearts out of a bottle and knocked them back.

'Ed, will you take me out?' she implored. 'Will you take me
somewhere nice for dinner?'

'Me?'

'I'm so alone.' Her voice trembled. 'I need to be with
someone.'

'Is your car outside?'

'Yes.'

'Go and wait in it. I'll be down in a minute.'

'Oh, thank you, Ed.' Her eyes brimmed with gratitude.

'Go on,' I said. 'I won't be long.'

She got up and swanned out.

I locked the door behind her and hurried over to the desk. One of
the biggest mistakes made by the wealthy is the blind faith they tend
to have in the impregnability of safes. A safe on the premises is an
open invitation to the cracksman. The more complex the combination and the thicker the steel the greater the challenge to the intrepid
'jool' thief. I once knew a bloke named Alvin Ostendorf who could
crack any combination safe or bank vault, as easily as opening a
can of sardines. He achieved fame some years ago when he opened
a massive vault, stuffed with microfilmed government secrets,
which had been built to withstand the explosion of a hydrogen
bomb. Alvin happened to be serving a ten stretch at the time having
been fingered by an unreliable associate. He was already a legend in
police circles and the underworld and was only sent for as a last
resort after all the experts including the manufacturers, had failed.
The trouble was that the time lock had gone berserk and had
advanced its setting by eight and a half years and unless something
was done would not open until 10.33 a.m on Wednesday 9th June
1980. How Alvin did it is not known and never will be. In exchange
for a free pardon from the Queen he had to sign the official secrets
act.

In the absence of a window box, the safest place to stash the
jewels was in the same place as my gun, under the loose floorboard next to the skirting behind the sofa.

CHAPTER NINE

Pru looked good behind the wheel of the Lamborghini. Strong black hair framing her pale oval face, damson-taloned fingers resting lightly on the gear shift and five hundred horsepower at the tip of her dainty right foot. I just hoped that the pills wouldn't give her the idea that she was a racing driver.

The car slid across the traffic-lights at Trafalgar Square and a half-inch pressure on the accelerator sent it hurtling up The Mall in the direction of Buckingham Palace. The Royal Standard fluttered regally at the top of the flag staff – our Queen was in residence.

Purring through the poshest part of town, in six or seven thousand quids worth of racy sports car, with a beautiful girl behind the wheel, is the stuff of which dreams are made. Men who get drunk all the time and behave badly, rarely get to first base with that kind of girl – I was tempted to pinch myself, but held back in case it woke me up.

She braked suddenly at a pedestrian crossing to let an old lady cross the road and a maroon sedan screeched to a halt a hair's breadth from our rear bumper. We jerked our heads around simultaneously.

The car behind was a Yankee job with English number plates, the kind of tool favoured by film stars and gangsters. The scowling pug behind the wheel was not a film star.

On the back seat of Pru's car was a crumpled garment that looked like a loose-fitting judo suit. She was certainly the kind of girl who might have to ward off the advances of lecherous men from time to time. I eyed her profile as we darted off again.

'Remind me not to get on the wrong side of you,' I said.

'What do you mean?'

I jerked a thumb over my shoulder.

'That's a judo outfit unless I'm very much mistaken.'

'Oh that,' she replied without interest. 'I'm learning karate, actually – I have a lesson every Thursday. It's a marvellous way of keeping fit and terribly slimming.'

'I'm sure it is,' I agreed. 'You any good at it?'

She dimpled fetchingly: 'I'd have no trouble laying you out!

Of course, it's more difficult with people who keep themselves in condition.'

She concentrated on her driving as we approached the Hyde Park Corner free for all, where five traffic jams meet in a bottleneck and it's every man for himself. The big American car was still on our *Daily Mail.*

'Where are you taking me?'

'The Renaissance. It's a perfectly divine little bistro in Chelsea – the *in* place and frightfully discreet. Simply everyone who is anyone goes there.'

I said: 'Sounds sexy,' and it was.

The walls of the restaurant were swathed in rich satin ruffles; the tablecloths were pink and a subdued glow filtered through table lampshades of the same material as the walls. It was like the inside of a Fortnum's chocolate box.

A wraith-like young man, with straggly shoulder-length hair and a face full of acne, minced over as we entered. He was informally dressed in trim slacks and a gondolier's blue and white striped T-shirt. He addressed Pru by name and enquired if, by the remotest chance, we'd booked a table. I shook my head glumly and slipped him a quid. He trousered the note and managed a smile.

'If you'll come this way, sir,' he lisped. 'I feel sure we may be able to find you a cosy little table for two.'

He led the way across the room and tucked us away in a remote corner – ideal for playing footsy. The gondolier dealt us menus and I ordered a couple of drinks.

Everybody who is anybody is always somebody that I would go to great lengths to avoid coming into contact with. But, as Pru had promised, they were there in strength. Vivid playgirls in shimmering evening gowns were shrieking and twittering on all sides. At the next table an adolescent girl in spectacles and too much makeup gazed in cow-eyed adoration at her escort, a richly tanned young man with very little chin. She might've been a runaway heiress with a Ward of Court writ slapped on her. Next to them a paunchy tycoon, in immaculate blue serge, was frantically groping a flighty young thing half his age. Things like that, between people like that, were going on all over the place.

The gondolier returned with the drinks and set them on the table.

I raised my glass to Pru and said: 'You come here with Sir Samford?'

'Our special place.' She hugged the words.

The familiar atmosphere seemed to cheer her up, though I was personally a bit anxious about how the alcohol was going to react when it reached her little tummy and found all those pills had got there first.

A nostalgic glow came into her eyes as she sipped her drink.

'Sammy and I came here the first night we met,' she said. 'We'd been wafted together at one of those milling drinks parties of Sophie Beauchamps'. She lets just anyone in, awful crude types she picks up on the race course. It was so marvellous to bump into someone civilized. We discovered that we had so much in common . . . and then we realized that it was going to be much more than that . . . much more.' Her eyes glazed over and a little, secret smile touched her lips. She was looking right through me and it was obvious that she could see Sir Samford on the other side – I resisted the temptation to glance over my shoulder.

'It may sound idiotic, but it was love at first sight. We became absolutely inseparable from the very first moment we met – weekends in Paris and in the country, the theatre, the opera, the ballet. We went everywhere together and we couldn't bear to be apart for a single evening.'

'Sounds like a TV commercial for herbal deodorant,' I said and snapped my fingers at the gondolier.

'Would you like to order, sir?' he lisped, pencil poised over his pad.

'Yeah, ' I pointed at my glass. 'Same again.'

'I was wondering if you were ready to order something to *eat*, sir.'

I threw my hands in the air in horror and smiled at Pru.

'What would you like?'

'*Ris de veau à la crème aux champignons*.'

'Same for me,' I said. 'And don't forget the drinks.'

The gondolier clucked disapprovingly and minced off.

'Refresh my memory,' I said when the drinks arrived. 'When

50

did you last see him?'

'I've already told you, Ed. Apart from that awful thing this morning, we had dinner together the night before he disappeared.' It came out a bit strained.

I couldn't recall whether or not she'd told me that before – I ticked myself off for the umpteenth time for not making notes.

Ris de veau à la crème aux champignons, when it arrived, looked as though a couple of pints of library paint had been spilt over it. Pru tucked in with relish. I ordered more whisky and got down to brass tacks.

'Look,' I said good-naturedly, 'if you expect me to track down Sir Samford you're going to have to tell me a lot more about him than what a truly wonderful human being he is.'

She snapped: 'What, for example?'

'I need to know more about the blackmail angle for a start,' I told her. 'Then I'd like to know a little more about his present financial position, who he owes gelt to and how much. What state of mind he was in when you last saw him and what terms he was on with his butler. . .'

'. . . You don't want much, do you?'

'Sonia and Patrick are making out that he's some kind of nut case.'

Pru's eyes flashed.

'Did they mention his debts? How foul and unfair. . . . Of course Sammy was in trouble. But it was Sonia and Patrick who were tightening the noose around his neck.' She lowered her voice to a whisper. 'We'd got a plan to escape them . . . a desperate plan. I want your solemn oath that you will never breathe a word of this to a living soul, Ed.'

I gave her my solemn oath, then swallowed a mouthful of library paint and killed the sickly taste of it with a gulp of whisky.

She leaned across the table and talked softly into my ear.

'It all started a year ago. Sammy is a real gambler, you know. One of the old school. He'd lay his life on the line for a bet.'

'Stakes don't come much higher than that,' I conceded.

'He gambled on simply anything, everything. He gambled with fate and his life was full of laughter and champagne.'

I couldn't allow her that one: 'I think you've already

mentioned all that. Tell me when Patrick Tomlinson joined the revellers – and when did he turn nasty?'

'I was telling you,' she said huffily. 'Sammy had given Giles Mountjoy, the stock-broker, twenty to one that the pomeranian would win at Crufts dog show. The stake was ten thousand, but for some inexplicable reason the judges chose the poodle. . . . The bet was entered in the betting book at Boodle's so the debt would have to be honoured. Sammy couldn't pay.'

'Cat person myself,' I remarked. 'Never have liked dogs. They bite.'

'He thought of selling Bramley Hall but that's mortgaged already. So is the Belgravia house. And most of the furniture and family jewels are in a sort of trust . . . they have to go to the heir, you see. He really didn't know which way to turn.'

'Bit of a tight corner.'

'Well, Sonia came up with the idea. It wasn't his sort of thing. He just wouldn't hear of it for ages. But in the end he gave in – dear God, I wish he hadn't!'

'Come on, let's have it.'

'It was very simple really. Red Knelly, that's Sammy's best race horse, was running in the 2.30 at Ascot that Saturday. There were five other runners but it was really a two horse race; Sammy told his jockey to pull up at the end, so the other horse won by half a length. He borrowed the money and backed the other horse. No one knew except Sonia. And Patrick who put the bet on for him. That was the beginning of the end. The swine has been blackmailing Sammy ever since.'

'The gee-gees have brought many a good man to his knees.'
Pru nodded passionately.

'I told him we'd got to think of something else. And that's why we started to devise the . . . desperate plan.'

'Desperate action was certainly called for.'

'You'll think us too awful for words. Ed . . . ' The scheming temptress was actually blushing.

'Go ahead. You'll feel a lot better with it off your chest.'

'We bought this little house up above Monte, in the hills.'

'If in doubt, keep spending.'

'Sammy sent Parkhurst over regularly with any valuables he could lay his hands on. He looked so trustworthy, no customs

52

officer would ever search him. You have absolutely no idea how difficult it is to transfer currency illegally nowadays, even if you can find anyone who will do it for you, they charge the earth – it almost pays you to go through the proper channels. Anyway, in a few months' time we were just going to disappear, and leave Patrick and Sonia holding the baby . . .'

CHAPTER TEN

Pru's bijou mews flat was tucked away in a quiet Knightsbridge cul-de-sac. There was one moderate sized room downstairs, off a tiny hall, and a short flight of stairs, painted daffodil yellow, went up to not more than two rooms above.

The downstairs room was neat, fluffy, silky, and sexy. The table-lamps had shades like extravagant hats. On the walls were prints by Andy Warhol and Graham Sutherland – I knew at once that she was anybody's.

She said: 'Do sit down,' and drifted over to a wood and chrome trolley on which there was an array of bottles.

I slumped into an armchair upholstered in glossy PVC and got attacked by the waxen tropical foliage of a potted plant that stood on a nearby tripod table.

'Hankey Bannister's?' she asked, indicating the drinks.

A noise upstairs pre-empted my reply.

'Good heavens,' Pru shrieked. 'What on earth was that?'

I put a finger to my lips, sprang to my feet and tiptoed to the door. My right hand slipped instinctively beneath the left lapel of my jacket and went to the place where once in a blue moon I carried my gun. It wasn't there.

I drew my metal watchstrap over a balled fist and slipped out into the hall. Keeping close to the wall I edged my way stealthily to the foot of the stairs. Pru appeared at the door of the sitting-room. She looked as though she was about to scream or faint.

I mouthed: 'Get back!' and waved her out of sight.

Upstairs a floorboard creaked.

Fighting off the overpowering desire to make a run for it, I stole up the stairs. A muffled footfall off to my right told me behind which door I would find the intruder. The door was ajar and it was dark inside except for the occasional beam of a flashlight. I moved to the side of the door and paused for thought. I could barge in throwing punches or hang about on the landing and grab him when he came out. I decided on the former.

I reached around the door jamb, snapped the light switch and threw myself into the room. An ape-like man, massively built, but without forehead or neck, whirled around from a bow-fronted chest of drawers in which he'd been rummaging.

'Tools Gunstone!' I yelped. 'What the hell are you doing here?'

His lips curled over strong nicotined teeth into a menacing smile.

'Wot's it to yuh, snooper?' he grunted.

And then he came at me with his head bent like a rampaging bull. The suddenness of the attack took me off guard and, before I could side-step, his bullet head had buried itself uncomfortably in my solar plexus. The air came out of me with the force of a burst tyre and I crumpled to my knees, winded. I rolled over sideways in the nick of time to save myself from a kick in the head. The boot whistled past my ear and he was off balance just long enough for me kick the other leg from under him. Tools' arms thrashed the air like a girl who's been pushed trying to keep her balance at the edge of a swimming pool, then he toppled over with a mighty crash.

It gave me the breather I needed. A moment later I was on my toes sparring. Tools lumbered to his feet and I fetched off a right hander that had started life at the balls of my feet. His nose exploded like a squashed tomato and the metal watch strap opened up a nasty gash beneath his left eye – blood sprang from the wound, rolled down his cheek and splattered onto the bedroom carpet.

I danced away from him with my dooks up, ready and willing to give him some more of the same.

Tools passed an enormous hand over his face, looked at the blood on it and said: 'That ain't fair, Ed. Yuh tripped me up when I weren't looking.'

'It's not very polite to poke about in a respectable young lady's drawers,' I said, breathing heavily.

'Diamonds set it up,' he groaned. ''E reckoned the Peveril tomfoolery was 'idden away somewhere in this gaff. A born tealeaf ain't gonna turn up 'is hooter at inside information like that is 'e? Not if 'e's in 'is right mind 'e ain't?'

He had a point at that.

Further conversation with Tools was averted by the sudden arrival of Pru. She came flying into the room shouting: 'What's that man doing dripping blood all over my bedroom carpet?' It was the fluffy sheepskin sort that moults all over your blue suit.

Something that might've been recognition flashed into Tools' eyes and his mouth gaped in amazement. Then he cast his eyes to the floor and sheepishly shuffled his feet.

'I didn't know it was your gaff, miss,' he mumbled. 'Straight up, I didn't. If I'd a known it was your gaff I was bustin' inter I wouldn't a done it, my life I wouldn't.'

'Just get out of here,' shrilled Pru. 'Get out of here this minute.'

Still mumbling apologies and dripping blood, Tools shambled out of the room, and went down the stairs with a heavy tread.

'Don't you want me to call the law?' I asked Pru.

'No,' she said, 'let him go.'

I dashed out of the room and shouted over the banister rail: 'Don't leave town, Tools – I'll be needing another word with you about this!'

His shoulders were hunched and his head bent. He was too crestfallen to reply, or even look around at me. He went out of the street door and closed it softly behind him.

I went back into the bedroom. Pru had got a flannel and a bowl of water from the bathroom and was sponging the blood off the carpet.

'What was that all about?'

She threw me a butter-wouldn't-melt look and said: 'What was what all about?'

'Come off it. Tools Gunstone seems to know you better than he knows the governor of Dartmoor prison.'

'Don't be ridiculous.' She rinsed the flannel out in the bowl and got to her feet. 'How would I know a lowlife like that?'

It was a good question.

'Tools gets around,' I said. 'If the Queen shelled out knight-hoods to cat burglars he'd've got one years ago. He's been a jewel thief by special appointment to the aristocracy for almost two decades. He knows his way around more stately homes than the geezer in charge of the National Trust.'

'I just felt rather sorry for him and he must've realized it – good heavens, look at your hand.'

I looked at my hand. The metal watch strap had done almost as much damage to it as it had to Tools. The knuckles were grazed and beginning to swell up and a jagged gash on my forehand was dripping more claret onto the carpet.

She hurried over with the bowl and placed it by my right foot to catch the blood, then dropped to her knees and got busy with the flannel.

I hadn't felt a thing until I'd seen the damage. All of a sudden needles of pain jabbed at my knuckles and it hurt like blazes.

'Hang on, I'll see to your hand in a minute,' said Pru, rubbing frantically at the blood-stained carpet. 'Oh dear, it's brand new from Habitat and cost a mint. I'll never get the stains out.'

'My watch is a write-off.'

A little later she led me by the elbow into the bathroom and gently bathed my hand in the wash basin.

She cleaned the wound: 'Nasty cut,' she commented, 'but I don't think it's as bad as it looks.'

'It was only a cheap watch strap,' I pointed out. 'Gangrene might set in and I'll have to have my hand off.'

She threw me a wicked little smile and reached down a bottle of iodine from the medicine cabinet.

'We can't allow that to happen,' she said, drawing the cork. 'I imagine you'd sue me for damages.'

I closed my eyes, clenched my teeth and waited for the pain. When it came it was a lot worse than I thought it was going to be.

'Ouch!' I yelped.

She pouted her lips at me and said: 'Come on, it isn't that bad. You're nothing but an overgrown baby.'

I grabbed a fist-full of hair at the nape of her neck with my good hand, jerked her head around and ground my mouth on hers. And then, as is liable to happen when a bedworthy young

56

lady tends the wounds of a hard-worked private eye, we repaired to the bedroom and one thing led swiftly to another.

I hate dreams, they're always about unattainable girls, or rotting in prison for twenty years for a crime of which I'm innocent, or starving to death in the gutter alone and unwanted. This one was about a man in black mask breaking into my office and knocking off the Peveril gems. It was so vivid it might easily have been prophetic – it awakened me with a nasty jolt.

As I slipped out of bed, Pru stirred in her sleep, murmured an inaudible endearment and cuddled the pillow. I hated leaving her, but a private eye who leaves a hundred thousand quids worth of tom unattended long enough to have a dream about a man in a black mask knocking it off, is a private eye who needs his head examined.

I dressed hurriedly and stole down the stairs. The wall clock in the sitting room said a quarter-past six, a good hour for catching worms, but less good for hangovers. I scribbled a quick note in biro on the telephone pad: 'Darling Pru, Thank you for a wonderful evening. Ring you later, love, Ed.' I added a couple of kisses and headed for the door. And then suddenly the phone rang. The shock cut a year off my life expectancy.

Curiosity got the better of my desire to make good my escape. I retraced my steps swiftly and silently and waited with my left hand resting lightly on the receiver. The bell rang on half a dozen times, then stopped. I gingerly lifted the receiver, placed a hand over the mouthpiece and put the other end to my ear.

PRU: (*Sleepily, on the bedroom extension*) Who on earth is it?
MAN: (*Thick Transylvanian accent – gravelly and muffled. Probably a disguised voice talking through a handkerchief*) Miz Pride, I know yuh gotta zee jewels – eef zay not return yoo die!
PRU: (*Shrill from fear*) What rot – Who-is-that?
MAN: (*Menacing*) Put zem in zee brown paper bag – take zem to zee Charing Crozz station – put zee brown paper bag in zee litter bin on zee platform zeven – eet eez zee Folkestone line . . .
PRU: (*Laughing*) Is this meant to be some kind of joke?
MAN: Eet eez no joke, Miz Pride – Yoo not obey, I keel you

57

wizout furzer notice − You make zee delivery twelve o'clock, not vone minute later − I votch you all zee time zo yoo not go to zee politz . . .

The mysterious caller rang off abruptly. I cradled the receiver, and tiptoed to the front door. I slipped out into the street as Pru came dashing out of her bedroom yelling: 'Ed, Ed! Where are you, Ed?' as though she was calling a dog.

CHAPTER ELEVEN

Discovering what I expected to discover when I got back to the office was no less vexing that it might've been if it'd come as a complete surprise. The door had been deftly jemmied and the room looked as though a pound or two of IRA gelignite had gone off in it. The drawers of my desk had been forced open and sinister letters from my bank manager and other documents of a confidential nature − like final demands from the telephone company and Electricity Board − littered the floor. The filing cabinet in which, apart from snotty handkerchiefs, rotting socks, dirty shirts and soiled Y fronts, I kept nothing of any value, had received the same treatment. Chairs were overturned, the telephone had been torn out of its socket and my trusty earthenware teapot was smashed to smithereens in a corner. But, most desolating of all, my lumpy old horsehair sofa had been disembowelled and its stuffing scattered about like curly locks on a barber-shop floor.

I could tell at a glance that the turnover was the work of a maladjusted vandal with more enthusiasm than talent. An expert would have been neater and more systematic in his search. The amateur ransacks; the professional is a craftsman. He knows that the most obvious hiding places are the best and there is no hiding place more obvious than a loose floor board. My pathetic visitor had left his callous stamp of disappointment and departed empty-handed.

A consuming impulse to grab the gems and have it away on my toes a bit lively overcame my usual caution. I made the

58

perilous omission of not securing the door behind me. No sooner had I knelt to lift the floor board than a swish like a skate on ice gave small warning of the blunt instrument that came into smart contact with the back of my skull. It made my head throb and my eyes water, but failed to spark me out. It had been the glancing blow of an inexperienced intruder, undoubtedly the same bloke who turned my gaff over. For a moment or two I stumbled about like a mis-fired rocket, then capsized into a corner clutching the back of my head. For a fleeting moment my vision cleared and I caught a glimpse of Patrick Tomlinson towering over me with a bar of iron in his hand. Then it rained blows and I fell down a manhole.

With the possible exception of drinking warm champagne there can be few worse ways of getting a splitting headache than being sapped by a novice. On no less than three occasions I'd been coshed by underworld experts and, like the one-punch cops from thirties gangster movies, each floored me with a single beautifully-aimed blow delivered with the correct amount of force to an area of my nut known medically as the *epicranial aponeurosis*. It is not, I hasten to add, an experience that I can warmly recommend. But if you've got to get clobbered you're a lot better off in the hands of a skilled technician.

I was out an hour and when I came to, I wished I hadn't. There were more lumps on my head than goose pimples on a topless barmaid's boobs. Trembling like an aspen leaf I got painfully to my feet and giddypaced across the room to my secret hidey-hole. The sparklers had gone missing, so had my shooter.

Somehow I got the overturned swivel chair upright and with a head full of exploding fireworks I slumped into it and cast a foggy eye around the demolished room. If I'd been able to feel anything, I'd've probably been able to burst into tears. But my senses were paralysed and I felt nothing. Not even self pity.

Time dragged by. I had neither the strength nor the inclination to move.

The first indication that I was going to live came an hour or so later, when the thought smote me that I hadn't a friend in the world. If I could think as clearly as that, there could be little doubt that I was already on the mend. I thanked heaven with a few choked sobs. Then the rickety old Victorian lift came up to my floor and footsteps approached the door. Someone knocked.

'Come in!' I croaked.

The door opened and Black Satin Hotpants slouched in, dressed for action in an orchid blouse and spiky-heeled Biba boots.

A streetwalker is rarely shocked by violence. She gets beaten black and blue by her pimp two or three nights a week and reverses the sado-masochistic process on kinky clients in revenge. The sight of me lolling in the chair like a rag doll stopped Hotpants in her tracks, but she didn't seem much surprised. A respectable girl would've run for her life screaming for the police.

She moved in for a closer look.

'You're bleeding,' she said.

'You ought to see the other bloke.' I tried to smile. It hurt. 'Fetch me some water.'

Wiggling all over, Hotpants pit-a-patted over to the wash basin in the corner and returned shortly with a cup of cold water and a damp rag. I took the cup from her and sipped gratefully while, without being asked, she dabbed tenderly at my wounds with the damp rag. I tried another smile. It still hurt. 'How did it happen?' she asked.

'I went into the Irish pub in Piccadilly and mentioned in passing that Oliver Cromwell was the finest Englishman that ever lived,' I said. 'The public bar was full of Orangemen.'

She said: 'Ask a silly question . . .' and laid the soothing damp rag on the back of my head, like a cold compress, over the worst of my bumps.

I continued the history lesson.

'I feel like Thomas De Quincey.'

'Who's he, when he's at home? One of Willy Paradis's mob?'

'No, he was a nineteenth-century opium-eater,' I explained. 'A golden-hearted hooker gave him a reviving drink when he was close to death on a Soho doorstep.'

'She needed her head examining. I've got no time for junkies.'

The cold compress felt good and my head slowly cleared.

'How come you know Willy Paradis?'

'Been around, ain't I? It's no wonder private eyes get their heads bashed in – THEY-ASK-TOO-MANY-QUESTIONS.'

'How did you know I was a private eye?'

'Says so on your door, don't it?' she sniggered.

'What brings you here today?'

'Business.'

'I thought so.' The smile hurt a little less this time. 'Sorry to disappoint you but I don't think I'm up to it.'

'Not *that* kind of business. I see there's a empty flat on the floor above and I was wondering who owns this block?'

'These premises are not residential,' I replied firmly. 'Business purposes only!'

'Business premises are just what I'm looking for, silly!'

'I need a drink.'

'Where's the bottle?' she asked, glancing around the room.

'Got smashed over my nut I expect.'

She dropped the wet rag on top of my head and patted me lightly on the cheek.

'I'll nip over to the supermarket,' she said and went bucketing out of the door.

'Whisky, if they've got it!' I shouted after her. 'Hankey Bannister's.'

'Okay!' she shouted back. 'Won't be a sec!'

All this shouting made my head hurt. She returned shortly with a bottle and poured three fingers into a plastic cup. I drank deeply and held out the cup for a refill. She replenished it and I quaffed again. The whisky went coursing through my veins like molten lead and it soon became clear that, if I played my cards right, or even if I didn't, there was an excellent possibility that I'd live long enough to die of lung cancer. She sat watching me.

'Stone me,' said Hotpants as I sipped my third drink. 'You don't half look a sight.'

'Thanks a lot,' I said and got unsteadily to my feet.

'You ought to pop round Charing Cross hospital casualty department and get patched up,' she suggested. 'You might have complications, like concussion or something.'

She sounded genuinely concerned for my welfare, but a lifelong fear of doctors prevented me from taking her advice.

61

'My brain's been addled since the day I was born.' I told her. 'A conk or two on the noggin is likely to knock more sense in than out.'

I shambled over to the wash basin, turned on the cold tap and splashed water on my face with both hands. When I'd patted myself dry with a hand towel and lit a cigarette I felt as well as I was going to that day.

'How about it then?' asked Hotpants as I poured myself another drink.

'How about what?'

'Putting in a word for me with the landlord so's he'll let me some business premises . . .?'

I crashed into the swivel chair and roared with laughter.

'Jesus Christ,' I managed to get out between guffaws. 'I bet you'd keep a dying man alive long enough to give him a knee trembler.'

'So what!' she snorted. 'A girl's got to keep her eye out for the main chance, ain't she?'

She sat on the edge of the desk and batted her eyelashes at me.

'If you put a word in for me I'll give you everything you've ever wanted from a woman,' she promised. 'Once a week free of charge.'

'It's a good offer,' I conceded. 'But property sharks in the West End have got enough to hide without taking on tenants who are going to bend the lease.'

'Okay, chicken. If you don't fancy giving me a reference, just put me in about who to phone and I'll do the rest.'

'I'll just bet you will,' I said. 'But if he tumbles you want a lumber gaff for French lessons he'll give you the slingers a bit lively.'

She snickered and took an eyebrow pencil and a well-thumbed address book out of her pigskin handbag.

'Come on what's the number?'

I sighed and grudgingly told her the estate agent's number. She licked the point of the eyebrow pencil with the tip of her tongue and scribbled it down in her address book.

'Whatever you do,' I pleaded, 'don't say I gave it to you.'

''Course not.' She minced over to the door and turned to give me a last look. 'Men!' she scoffed with a cheeky smile. 'When they're hard they're soft, and when they're soft they're hard.' She puckered her lips prettily, blew me a kiss and went out.

CHAPTER TWELVE

With the bottle in one hand and my shaving mirror in the other I reclined in the swivel chair and made a close examination of the damage to my battered noddle. There were four or five bumps that I could see, and a few more around the back that I couldn't. The injuries sustained were not as extensive or as serious as they might've been. I took a swig from the bottle, then set it down on the desk and felt the bumps gingerly with the tips of my fingers. They seemed to be the size of quail eggs but felt like ostrich eggs. There was no mistaking the pain; it pounded around in my skull like a six months' accumulation of monumental hangovers.

The face in the mirror was pale and grim and brooding. It had plenty to brood about. I'd broken my golden rule and allowed myself to be dragged in on a murder investigation. I wasn't any good at it and the sooner I got back to a bit of wholesome divorce-snooping the better. I was lucky to be alive.

'Tell you what,' I said. 'I'll ring Pru and hand in my notice.'

A look of utter contempt came into the eyes in the mirror.

'What? And leave a lovely defenceless girl in the lurch?' they seemed to say. 'Have a heart! You can't pay back her two-and-a-half anyway.'

'How very true,' I sighed.

'And what about getting your own back on Tomlinson? If someone caves your skull in you are supposed to do something about it.'

'I know, I know.'

'Well, are you going to let the swine get away with it scot-free?'

I lurched to my feet and cried: 'Not bloody likely.'

Later, I popped around to the 24-hour chemist in Piccadilly Circus to buy a bottle of witch-hazel and a phial of Veganin. I knew neither would bring much comfort to my aching head. For cracked skulls, hangovers and broken hearts time is the only healer.

On my way back to the office I ducked into a callbox and phoned Tangerine. Tangerine was a camp young queen with yellow hair and so many convictions for importuning, that she'd been forced to give up hawking her mutton on the the meat rack under the arches in Piccadilly Circus and now did char-ing at 75p an hour when she couldn't find work posing suggestively for gay porno mags. She loved me with a passion that was far from pure and was madly keen to get into my Y-fronts. But she knew I'd scream if she laid a finger on me so she confined her naughty little advances to relating explicit details of her exploits in the bilges of homosexual society, as she flitted around the office with a feather duster once a fortnight. Somewhere in the back of her devious mind lurked the hope that one day she'd turn me on. Like most ginger beers she was frightened, lonely, disillusioned and beset.

The phone rang seven bells before her lisping cadences came on the line.

'Don't just breathe,' she cried into my ear. 'Speak to me.'

I said: 'Say please.'

'*Please*,' she trilled, putting suggestive emphasis to the word.

'It's Ed,' I said. 'Ed Nelson.'

'Thank God. I thought it was another of those phantom heavy breathers with delicious fantasies about what they'd like to do to me. Heaven knows who they are; all they do is breathe – then hang up without saying a word.'

'Some people have all the luck.'

'Ooo, you are wicked,' she said. 'What can I do for you – ask simply *anything*?'

I switched on the most fetching voice I could muster.

'My gaff's been turned over – the whole place is upside-down. I was wondering if you'd mind running your feather duster over it?'

'What an absolutely thrilling life you do lead, ducky.' She let out a filthy little laugh. 'I'll scamper around just as fast as my tiny feet can carry me.'

'You're an angel. The lock's busted so you won't need a key.'

'I love you, Ed,' she said. 'I really do.'

'Listen,' I said, lowering my voice. 'I've got to drive down to the country – I'll give you a ring as soon as I get back. If you don't hear from me by tomorrow morning, phone the Yard, ask for Superintendent Clews and tell him that he'll find my corpse at Bramley Hall. He'll know what you mean.'

'I've come over all of a flutter.'

'Don't get your knickers in a twist,' I said and cradled the receiver.

I dialled the operator and asked her to connect me with the telephone engineers. She said she couldn't do it. I asked her why not and told her it was urgent. She said it wasn't her job to put people through to the engineers and she wouldn't do it and told me to try information. I dialled information and asked to be put through to the engineers; another girl told me she couldn't do it. I told her I was blind; she said she was sorry about that, but the best she could do was give me their number. I dialled it and waited. It rang interminably. I fumbled a cigarette from a crushed packet and set light to it with a safety match.

In the fullness of time the engineer came on the line and I told him my phone was out of order. He said that a maintenance man would be along to fix it sometime towards the end of the week or the beginning of next. I gave him my number and mentioned in passing that without a phone I was out of business; he said he couldn't help that. I told him that the country was going to the dogs; he agreed and hung up on me loudly.

I fumbled in my pocket for another 2p, couldn't find one and balanced a florin over the slot. I dialled Pru's number and toyed again with the idea of giving her the slingers.

'Ed!' she shrieked. 'How could you leave me like that, without saying a word? I've been trying to get you all the morning.'

'It's only ten-thirty,' I said. 'I left you a note.'

There was a tense silence and when she spoke again it sounded like she'd lost her bottle.

'Someone's threatening to kill me. He woke me up at the crack of dawn and started threatening me down the phone . . . A man with a thick foreign accent. He thinks I've got the jewels and if I don't hand them over to him he is going to kill me.'

'Was it a Transylvanian accent, by any chance?'

'How the hell should I know?' she snapped. 'Middle European, I'd say.'

I said: 'I see.'

'He must be an accomplice of the beast we caught rummaging around in my bedroom last night.'

'Tools Gunstone?' I laughed.

'I fail to see what you find so amusing about it.'

'Sorry,' I said and stifled my laughter. 'All Tools does is what Diamonds Silverman tells him to do – he wouldn't know how to recruit an accomplice if his life depended on it.'

'Why not?'

'Because he's a congenital idiot.'

If I'd been in the same room with her she'd've hit me over the nut with a blunt instrument.

'If the underworld think I have Sammy's jewels,' she blazed, 'something terrible is going to happen to me – I just know it will.'

'How do you know?'

'I just know, that's all. Don't you even know how the criminal mind works?'

If I'd been feeling up to it, I would've been pretty upset by a crack like that, but I wasn't feeling up to it.

'The papers are saying that Sammy did it and stole the jewels himself,' she went on. 'The police seem to be of the same opinion and so are all the thieves and gangsters in London.'

'Well,' I sighed, 'they are wrong.'

'How do you know?'

'Because I had them.'

'You!' she hollered. 'You mean *you* stole them?'

'Don't do your nut. I didn't knock them off exactly. You may remember that you suggested I should pop round to the Peveril place yesterday?'

'So what?'

'So, I just happened to come upon them in a bust of Shelley.'

'Shelley!' she shrieked. 'Shelley? – I don't believe you.'

'Suit yourself,' I said. 'But there's a bust of him in the library and the family sparklers were hidden inside it.'

She fell silent for a moment or two to let it sink in and when next she spoke her tone was almost apologetic.

'Why on earth didn't you tell me that last night?'

'Wasn't sure I could trust you.'

'You have to be careful, I suppose,' she admitted generously. 'So now you've got them, have you?'

'Not any more.'

'How much did you get for them?'

'I didn't flog them,' I said. 'I only wish I had.'

Across the miles of telephone wire that separated us I could feel her disbelief.

'Where are they then?'

'Good question,' I said. 'As a matter of fact that's what I rang you about – if you will now let me get a word in edgeways.'

She took a sharp intake of breath.

'Go on.'

'I got a nasty premonition in the early hours of the morning,' I explained. 'I realise that it was impolite, but I had to nip out of bed a bit lively and hurry back to the office to see if the gems were still where I stashed them. When I got there I found that some maniac had torn the place apart and just as I took a gander to see if the jewels had gone missing, your friend Tomlinson bounced an iron bar off my nut a few times. When I came to the cupboard was bare.'

'I knew it was him,' she exploded. 'I knew it was him all along.'

'Don't blow your cool,' I warned. 'We can't pin anything on him yet.'

'Why not?'

'It'll be his word against mine and my word doesn't count for much with old Clews at the moment,' I said. 'What we've got to do is capture him bang to rights with the tomfoolery in his sky rocket.'

'I do wish you'd speak English.'

I ignored that and lit another cigarette.

'You'd better go down to Bramley Hall then,' she continued hesitantly.

'I know.'

I groaned.

'The sooner the better – he might do a bunk.' Her voice was insistent. 'If, as you say, we capture him 'bang to rights with the tomfoolery in his sky rocket,' the police will have to believe us and Sammy will be able to come out of hiding.'

'What's all this *we*?' I asked. 'Its *me* who keeps on taking all the risks.'

'I thought that was supposed to be your line of business.'

'I've got a good mind to chuck this case up, Miss Pride,' I came back to her sharply. 'Murder investigations aren't up my street, they make me nervous . . .'

'Don't say that, Ed! Didn't last night mean anything to you at all?'

'It meant a great deal to me,' I assured her. 'That's why I wouldn't mind being around long enough for a second performance.'

She tried a different tack.

'Alright,' she said, 'if you feel like that about it you can return my two-hundred and fifty pounds by the lunch-time post.'

That hurt.

'Alright,' I grumbled. 'I'll go down to Bramley-sodding-Hall. But if I get done in I'll come back and haunt you for the rest of my life.'

'I'll see you get plenty of protection, sweetheart,' she cooed and hung up.

What the hell did she mean by that?

CHAPTER THIRTEEN

My stout-hearted 1100 was nothing if not game. A geriatric among mass-produced cars (thirteen last birthday), the miles on her clock reached three times around the world and some to spare. It was asking a good deal of her to make a wild dash to the country with her speedometer, at times, touching seventy.

Apart from getting snarled up in a spaghetti junction some-where along the way – dual carriageways whizzing off it in all directions, furiously going nowhere – it looked as though the old girl was going to get us to our destination before the sands of time ran out on her altogether. Four or five miles from the Peveril pile, minus a hubcap and a door handle that had shaken off from vibration, I suddenly caught sight of an olive green saloon in the rear-veiw mirror. It was coming up fast and in less than a minute was on my tail.

I'd turned off the main drag a mile or two back and was winding my way along the perilously narrow country lanes. I'd rather drive drunk around Hyde Park Corner in the rush hour than chance my arm with rural traffic around the hairpin bends of England's green and pleasant land.

The lunatic on my tail blasted his horn and weaved from side to side inches from my rear bumper. My shoulders began to sweat. 'Roadhog,' I muttered and stabbed the accelerator. But the faster I went the faster he went and, for something under a mile, we careered along, nose to tail, like a switch-back joy-ride.

Near a farmhouse with a bed and breakfast sign outside, the road widened a little. I hugged the mossy bank on my near side, stuck my hand out of the window and vigorously waved him on. He pulled alongside and for an instant I caught sight of the driver — an army sergeant in a peaked cap, remodelled in the aggressive style favoured by the SS during the war. The peak was cut back so that it came down vertically over the forehead and covered the eyes like a visor. It looked as though he was going to overtake me. Then, at the last minute, perhaps over-excited by the thrill of the chase, he pulled over sharply and rammed me amidships. The steering wheel spun in my hands and the car rebounded wildly from bank to bank like a ricocheting bullet. I threw on the anchors instinctively, and ended up in a tyre-smoking front-wheel skid that sent the car into a giddy two-and-a-half turn spin until it faced the way we'd come.

The green saloon had fallen back and for a moment or two we sat face to face wondering what to do for an encore. The sergeant took the initiative, as one would expect, and came at me fast like a berserk tank. Frozen with fright, and powerless to do anything about it, I sat there wondering what on earth I'd done to upset the army — all I could come up with was the favour I'd done them by refusing to be tempted by their glossy ads to join up.

The impact when it came was sickening and it threw such a

69

fright into the old girl that she reared up like a shying horse and leapt headlong through the hedgerow, landing lumpishly in a slimy ditch – it was a natural reaction. The rest that happened was God's vengeance on me for drinking, smoking and going to bed with girls. The windscreen shattered and a fragment of flying glass sliced a slug of flesh out of my chin; the steering column clouted me savagely about the chest and the indicator flipper disappeared up my left nostril.

The olive green saloon let out a triumphant fanfare on its horn and with a roar of its V8 engine made off at speed, like a victorious gladiator. Winded and dripping blood from my chin, I eased myself gingerly out of the car; I slumped down on a carpet of wild flowers under a nearby oak tree. Knitting my brows, I gazed mournfully at my faithful red roadster. Her bonnet was completely stove in, her front wheels were buckled and bandy and the gleam of her wind-screen had turned into the black hole of Calcutta. She was the kind of wreck that St John's ambulance men take corpses out of.

There are days when nothing seems to go right, and you end up wishing that you'd never got out of bed. This had the makings of just such a day and it was only just past noon. I'd suffered head injuries at the hands of a footpad and come close to the grave in a spectacular car crash.

I staunched the wound on my chin with my handkerchief, smoked a crumpled cigarette and then, with waves of pain washing over me, made my way to the nearby farmhouse.

The ample, florid-faced country woman was smiling when she came to the door, but her face slumped the moment she laid eyes on me and she let out an involuntary yelp of surprise.

'Had a bit of an accident,' I explained. 'Car came off the road.'

'Gracious me,' she cried, 'shall I call an ambulance?'

'No thanks,' I said. 'They'll only X-ray my chest and tell me I've got lung cancer.'

A bewildered expression passed over her face but it turned slowly into a sympathetic smile.

'Come inside,' she said. 'Come inside and sit yourself down.'

She opened the door wide and I went past her into a whitewashed hall with a grandfather clock in the corner, a

70

barometer on one wall and on another a stern warning in a rosewood frame:

> GOD is the HEAD of this HOUSE.
> The UNSEEN guest at every meal.
> The SILENT listener to every
> CONVERSATION.

'You sure you'm alright, sir?' she enquired as she led me across the hall and out into the large, boiled-cabbage-smelling kitchen at the back of the house.

I said: 'I've felt worse,' and slumped heavily into a wooden chair.

'You look like you could do with some hot sweet tea,' she said.

'I could also do with getting my brains tested.'

'Would you like a dressing on that nasty cut, sir?' she asked as she handed me the cup.

I removed the handkerchief and showed her my chin.

Her tongue clucked the roof of her mouth while she inspected the wound, and then she hurried over to the sink and returned shortly with a bowl of water, a flannel and a bottle of TCP.

It was my day for getting patched up by ladies.

When she'd administered the first aid and I'd drunk two cups of tea and smoked three cigarettes Mrs Pinkrose – as she identified herself – went out to find her husband and tell him to yank my wrecked car out of the five-acre field.

In fact he put himself out even further. It's a mystery to me why country folk indulge in so much uncalled-for generosity – they don't know any better I suppose – but he actually towed it down to the village garage and when I finally felt fit enough to leave, his wife refused my offer of payment.

Mr Goodway, the proprietor of the village garage, was a beefy individual with a beer gut. He had on a very greasy boiler suit and there was more grease on his hands and face. I took him to be in his middle forties. A grin rippled over his face as I entered his workshop – it was the grin of the honest car dealer. I knew instinctively that my faith in human nature was about to be restored.

' 'Morning,' I said as brightly as I could muster. 'I believe my car is here?'

The grin rippled again, as a breeze ruffles the surface of a pond.

Mr Goodway said: 'Mornin', zur. What's left of 'er be 'ere right enough – she'm a write off, I reckon, zur.'

My lips twitched, but I would've sworn it was St Vitus dance if anyone'd accused me of a smile.

'Sure you can't fix it?'

'What be yuh insurance cover, zur?'

'Third party.'

'Bain't worth it unless yuh got full comprehensive,' he said. 'Cost yuh less to buy a new one.'

I tried out my most persuasive tone of voice.

'Surely you can do something to get it back on the road?'

He spread his hands in a gesture of hopelessness and gravely shook his head.

'She be an ole banger, zur,' he replied mournfully. 'Best I can do is take 'er off yuh 'ands for scrap.'

I said: 'No,' and made as if to stalk out.

''Old 'ard, zur,' he cried. 'It be a long job – cost yuh more'n a new one, like I say. If'n yuh come back in a week maybe I can do sumthin' with her – but I make no promises, mind.'

'I know she's pretty banged up,' I said. 'But you look like a mechanic with hands like a surgeon.'

Everyone is a sucker for flattery and car dealers are no exception. He beamed with pride.

'Do me best, zur,' he said.

'Can you rent me a car in the meantime?' My voice was slightly over-anxious.

The shrewd smile returned once more, but on this occasion Mr Goodway had the good grace to hide it behind his hand.

'I can let yuh 'ave a 'Illman Avenger, zur,' he said. 'Five pounds a day and three pence a mile.'

I said: 'It's a deal.'

CHAPTER FOURTEEN

Bramley Hall lay only eight miles away from the village where I had hired the car. I paused at the local to take aboard two double whiskies and an egg and tomato roll, then hit the road. Fifteen minutes after I'd started out I was driving through the wrought-iron gates. In the drive I came upon Elinor, carrying a wicker basket brimming with enough flowers for a king's funeral. She was deep in conversation with a gnarled yokel. I drew up beside them and alighted from the car.

'That really is most frightfully kind of you, Mr Tidmarsh,' Elinor was telling the yokel. 'I am most terribly grateful to you.'

''Tweren't nuthin', mum,' Mr Tidmarsh grovelled. 'Oi'll spread some 'orse muck on yuh rose bed sarternoon, an' water 'em 'olly'ocks an' 'ybrid trolliuses afore I goes 'ome fer me tea.'

'Oh, thank you so very much, Mr Tidmarsh. What an absolute treasure you are.'

His cracked old face wreathed in smiles, Mr Tidmarsh tugged respectfully at his forelock.

'If'n the weather do 'old,' he remarked, flicking his lizard-like eyes to the sky, 'oi'll weed thar chrysanthemums.'

'Oh, Mr Tidmarsh, heaven only knows what I'd do without you . . . . You really are most fearfully kind. . . . Thank you most awfully.'

Elinor turned to see who I was. She gave a little start. Then smiled at me. 'All that a chrysanthemum asks for in the summer is to be free from weeds and have moisture when necessary,' she said.

I returned her smile and nodded my agreement.

'They're almost human,' I commented.

Mr Tidmarsh tugged his forelock once more and slunk off behind a conical-shaped juniper bush.

Elinor gave me a more careful inspection and said: 'Goodness me, Mr umerrr . . . What in the world has been happening to you?'

'Nelson,' I replied, 'Ed Nelson. I'm the private investigator from London – I crashed my car and I feel like the Wreck of the Hesperus.'

'I remember now,' Elinor said. 'You're that gumshoe who

paid us a visit the other day, aren't you?'

I grinned at her broadly and nodded.

'Sure you weren't sapped?'

'Sapped?'

'Isn't *sapped* what they call it when you are struck over the head with a blunt instrument?'

'It certainly is,' I agreed. 'I was just wondering where you picked up such words.'

'Whodunnits,' she replied. 'Reading trash is my favourite vice – I simply devour them.'

'I'd rather like to have a word with Patrick Tomlinson.' I tried to sound casual and failed. 'Any idea where I might find him?'

'I don't think I've seen him today. Now that you mention it, I don't think I saw him yesterday either.'

'What about Lady Sonia?' I asked. 'Is she around?'

'Actually, I believe that she popped in to Silchester to have lunch with the rural dean.' She gave me an impish smile. 'Sonia loves being on committees – she's raised pots of money for her pet charities. She's so frightfully good at making passionate appeals.'

There was a little dagger of sarcasm in Elinor's voice that left me in no doubt that she was a good deal less green than she was cabbage-looking.

'What time are you expecting her back?'

'No idea, Mr Nelson,' she said. 'No idea at all.'

'Do you mind if I wait?'

'Please do by all means.'

She bent down and tugged a large weed out of the border. Then, giving me a curt nod, she set off up the drive at a smart trot, leaving a trail of flowers in her wake.

I leant against the car, lit a fag, looked up at the house and wondered where the charming Patrick had stashed the jewels. With him and Sonia out of the way this seemed like a heaven-sent opportunity to turn the drum over, but turning over a place that size would take a month of Sundays. When the cigarette was spent, I drove up to the front door, cut the engine and got out of the car.

There seemed to be no one about. With butterflies flapping about in the region of my solar plexus, I crunched across the

74

gravel to the front door. As I reached for the handle, there came a low whistle from a nearby holly bush. I jumped out of my skin.

The leaves rustled and Elinor's head craned around the side in its unmistakable floppy hat.

'Psst,' she went and beckoned to me with a crooked finger. 'Psst, psst,' then the finger went to her lips and she ducked out of sight behind the Christmas decorations.

'We can't talk here,' she informed me, in a stage whisper, as I reached her side. 'We might be overheard, follow me.'

She jerked her head sideways and crouching low headed off along the herbaceous border.

'Keep down,' she hissed. 'The tree peonies don't give much cover.' I tagged along behind her, mystified, and bent double like an Indian scout.

We fetched up eventually at a broken-down summer house, in a secluded corner of the garden, with a bed of nettles in the doorway. Elinor nipped over them lightly and disappeared inside. I followed more gingerly. Blinking at the sudden gloom, I found her sitting on a rustic bench.

'We're safe here,' she said beaming. 'No one ever comes near this old summer house.' I sat down beside her hoping she wasn't the homicidal maniac who'd bumped off Parkhurst.

'I had to talk to you,' she went on breathlessly. 'I know that everyone is under suspicion now. But you can rule out James. I can tell you all about it.'

'Who on earth's James?'

'My son,' rasped Elinor.

'Good Lord!' I said. 'Nobody mentioned that you had a son.' She tossed her floppy brim contemptuously.

'Well, I'm telling you now.' She sounded rather cross.

'I expect you are wondering why I live here like a poor relation.' It hadn't even crossed my mind. 'Well, I am a poor relation. My husband died and left me without a bean. James was only two then, and Samford let me come and live here. The only thing that I know anything about is gardening and he said it would be nice if I looked after the gardens. That was twenty years ago and James – he's Samford's heir, you know, Samford having no children, so all this is terribly *important* to him – he's gone into insurance broking in the city.'

She paused for breath. 'Glad you told me all this,' I said encouragingly. 'It's the kind of thing that can look dead dodgy if a private detective uncovers it for himself.'

She gave me a canny smile and said: 'I may look an old fool but I keep my ears open and I know what's going on. Samford has been selling anything of value that he could lay his hands on, unloading all the heirlooms and everything that should come to James. He'd just get Parkhurst to pop them in a body belt and take them out of the country for him; Parkhurst had made lots of little trips to France and every time something else disappeared. I shouldn't think there's anything of any value left by now. I'm not saying it was all Samford's fault; his life style's always been very grand. What with his gambling debts and one thing and another he has always needed quite a lot of money just to keep his head above water – and then of course there is the upkeep of two houses and his stud farm.

'Anyway, I told James that he would simply have to do something before there was absolutely nothing left for him to inherit. So he went round to the London house to see Samford. But he was out and while he was waiting for him to come back he began noticing just how many things were missing and he remarked on it to Parkhurst. You can't imagine what happened – Parkhurst went quite mad; he got into this maniacal rage and threw James bodily out of the house . . . Now, the one thing I don't want is for anyone to suspect James . . .'

'Perish the thought,' I said.

Her eyes darted in my direction appealingly.

'You can see that he couldn't have done it, don't you, Mr Nelson?'

I was trying hard, but she was protesting just a little too much. Now she'd marked my card about the lad I hadn't even known existed, he sounded like he had plenty going for him in the way of a motive. Tomlinson was still my favourite suspect though.

Our illuminating little chat didn't last long after that. She suddenly remembered that she'd forgotten to put her flowers in water and dashed off to see to them.

As Sonia wasn't due back for a while and I'd lost interest in searching the house, I decided to take a walk through the home

76

wood in the hope that a little fresh air would relieve the stabbing pains that still jabbed at my skull.

The walk was nice until I got some distance into the wood. The leaves became thick over my head like a curtain over the sun. The spongy bed of leafmould beneath my feet gave off a dank, musty odour as my shuffling tread disturbed the top layer. Small dark birds (thrushes, perhaps, or sparrows) flitted from bough to bough like bats. Pausing only for a moment, to relieve myself against a tree, I hurried through the wood. In an effort to allay my fears, I whistled softly to myself.

I'd almost made it to the other side when suddenly a screaming pheasant took off at my feet and frightened me out of a year's growth. It was an unnerving place and I was thankful to get it behind me as I emerged once more into the sunshine and open countryside.

To be accurate the terrain on the far side of the wood was a good deal more rough than open. Ahead of me lay an expanse of wasteland, thick with gorse bushes and parched bracken. After that there was what looked like a disused slate quarry.

A distant steeple-clock struck two. If Lady Sonia's lunch date with the rural dean had been at one, she'd need rather longer than an hour to outline her latest 'passionate appeal'. I decided to skirt around the slate quarry and try to find an alternative route back to the house avoiding the spooky wood.

The wasteland was littered with discarded beer cans, Coca-Cola bottles, plastic cups, sandwich wrappers and crumpled newspapers – the hallmark of untidy picnickers. Dangling from a branch of a secluded gorse bush was a used French letter – evidence that one couple at least had been influenced by the campaign for birth control, even if the slogan 'KEEP BRITAIN TIDY' had not yet sunk in.

At the edge of the slate quarry I sat down on the grass and lit a cigarette. It was a hot afternoon and I was swimming in sweat. I struggled out of my jacket, placed it on the grass at my side and loosened my tie.

The quarry was as deep as a church spire is high and I wondered idly, as I peered over the edge, how long it had taken to dig. Then suddenly, on a wide ledge, about twenty-five feet below I saw something that froze my blood and dried my spit. It

77

was something that looked like the body of a man.

My mouth gaped and the cigarette plummeted downwards, leaving a shower of tiny sparks in its wake. To avoid following it when I fainted, I flattened myself on the ground. When my head had stopped swimming, I opened my eyes and forced myself to take another look.

It lay face up; its features were hideously contorted and its wide pool-of-blood eyes were staring up at me. One leg was folded under the trunk of the body and the other dangled over the ledge, swaying listlessly to and fro like a pendulum. Then, through the beads of sweat that poured down my face and filled my eyes, I saw who it was.

I rolled away from the edge and cried aloud: 'Blimey O'Reilly, it's Patrick Tomlinson!'

CHAPTER FIFTEEN

'What's that you say?' Clews, as I'd expected, was very far from pleased to receive the news of Tomlinson's demise. He was extremely angry, shouting at me. 'Would you kindly explain to me why it is that bodies keep popping up everywhere you go?'

I winced and jerked the receiver an inch or two away from my ear.

'It's as big a mystery to me as it is to you, Super,' I bleated. 'Honestly it is . . . I went for a stroll around the estate, just as I've told you, and there he was dead as a door nail in the slate quarry. I'm as sick of things like that happening to me as you are.'

'How do you know he's dead?' he blazed. 'Did you touch him?'

'No, no,' I cried. 'I didn't touch anything – corpses are nasty cold things and I wouldn't dream of laying a finger on one. I did think of climbing down for a closer butchers, but I couldn't find any rope – and smoking forty Senior Service a day is not exactly the right kind of training for rock-climbing.'

'Have you informed the local constabulary?'

'No, I thought you'd like to be the first to know.'

'Alright,' groaned Clews. 'Remain where you are, touch nothing and speak to no one. I'm on my way down.'

'Shall I phone the local nick?'

'No,' he snapped and hung up.

Elinor, who had been standing at my elbow throughout the telephone conversation, stared at me with wide tortured eyes and said: 'Beastly business, what a beastly business – first poor Dartmoor is murdered . . .'

'Parkhurst.'

'Yes, of course, how silly of me, Parkhurst. Then Patrick is murdered and dear Samford is missing – I can't help wondering which of us is going to be next.'

'We don't yet know for certain if Patrick Tomlinson was *murdered*. There's always the possibility that he slipped and fell.'

Elinor wandered off aimlessly in the direction of the drawing-room. I trailed along behind her. She paused at the door and gave me a backward glance.

'You don't really believe that, do you, Mr Nelson?'

'No, not really.'

It crossed my mind that Elinor might've done him in herself. After all, it did seem a bit fishy that she hadn't even mentioned the Sonia and Tomlinson angle in the summer house and she'd taken her time in getting around to telling me all that guff about James. What with all the gardening she was probably a wiry old bird and quite strong enough to shove a bloke over a precipice – even a feeble old lady could shove a bloke over a precipice if he happened to have his back to her. But on the spur of the moment I couldn't think up a good enough motive.

Ten minutes later Lady Sonia soft-shoed into the room with a brightly coloured Hermes scarf knotted under her chin.

I got to my feet.

'What are you doing here?' she demanded in a voice as taut as wire.

I made no reply.

'Oh, Sonia,' cried Elinor, 'something unspeakably dreadful has happened.'

Sonia looked right into me.

I cast my eyes to the ground and noticed that there was sand on her shoes.

'Mr Tomlinson's had an accident.' I brought my eyes up to meet hers. 'He has fallen or may have been pushed . . . into the slate quarry.'

Tears welled up into her eyes. She opened her mouth to speak but no words came out. She buried her face in her hands and slumped onto the chintz sofa next to Elinor. Sonia began to cry, just a little at first, then gradually her whole body began to shake and the tears bucketed as freely as rain at a test match. Elinor placed a hand on her shoulder in an effort to comfort her. Her grief certainly seemed genuine enough.

'He's done it again,' she moaned, between choked sobs. 'He's done it again.'

'Who, who?' I asked urgently. 'Who has done it again?'

A siren licked up the drive and through the window. Across the green acres of parkland, a police car loomed into view.

Sonia took her hands from her face and gazed blankly out of the window.

'*Who* has done it again?' I repeated desperately.

I might as well have been talking to a brick wall.

The police car slithered to a halt outside the front door and disgorged four uniformed cops from the local nick, an inspector, two constables and a sergeant. The ladies having come unglued by shock and grief, I hurried to the front door and opened it to the cops.

The inspector, a florid faced, heavily-built man of arresting ugliness, stepped across the threshold, without so much as a by your leave and barged by me into the hall. If it'd been my house I'd've asked to see a search warrant. In ordinary circumstances I might well have asked to see a search warrant, whether it was my house or not, but the reason for their visit was far from ordinary, and it didn't seem like a good idea to put their backs up.

'Your name Nelson?' snapped the inspector.

'Mr Nelson.' I looked him straight in the eye. 'Mr Nelson is my name. I'm a private investigator from London.'

'I know all about you,' sneered the inspector. 'Superintendent

Clews has instructed me to see that you remain here until he arrives.'

'I wasn't thinking of going anywhere,' I sneered back at him.

'Where's the body?'

'It seemed rather bulky.' I eyed him coolly. 'So I left it where I found it.'

'In the slate quarry?

'Right.'

'Where's the slate quarry?'

I pointed across the lawn towards the wood.

'Through those trees.'

'Sergeant Mothersole, constable Sorenson!' The inspector barked at his subordinates. 'You two go to the slate quarry and find the body, but for goodness sake don't touch anything until the forensic squad arrives.'

Sergeant Mothersole leapt to attention and saluted smartly.

'Sar!' he clipped.

'Want me to show them where it is?' I enquired.

'No, you stay here where I can keep an eye on you.' The inspector looked daggers at me for an instant then flicked an eyeball at the sergeant. 'Get going, Mothersole, and find the corpse.'

The sergeant saluted a second time and set off, lef-ri-lef-ri-lef, across the lawn with constable Sorenson in hot pursuit.

The inspector issued a final instruction to the remaining officer. 'Constable Dewsbury, stand guard on the door and let no one in or out.'

Clinging to each other for dear life, Lady Sonia and Elinor came timidly to the drawing-room door and gave the inspector an empty stare. Sonia looked none too good. Her make-up was spread over her face in an ugly smear – green eye-shadow, scarlet lipstick, pink pancake and mascara ran together like paint on an artist's palette. She tried a smile but it came out twisted and sour.

The inspector touched the peak of his braided cap.

'Lady Sonia Peveril?'

'Yes,' she choked.

'Inspector Sherman of the Silchester constabulary, madam,' he explained respectfully. 'Superintendent Clews has instructed

81

me to take charge pending his imminent arrival. My orders are that no one is to leave the house and that the body is to remain where it is until further notice.'

Sonia stood stiff and still for several seconds then let out a dreadful, spine-chilling scream and broke away from Elinor's embrace.

'I can't bear it!' she shrilled and dashed across the hall and up the staircase. Half way up she paused and rounded on the company below. 'There's a homicidal maniac at large! Why don't you go out and hunt him down instead of loitering in my hall?'

CHAPTER SIXTEEN

Lofty Clews stood at the edge of the slate quarry, looking down at the corpse of Patrick Tomlinson. He was flanked by the burly pathologist, Professor Lionel Green-Parker, and detective sergeant Algernon du Ponte. They too were gazing over the edge.

In the clearing between the fringe of the woods and the edge of the quarry a dozen or so uniformed policemen were poking about in the undergrowth with long sticks. They were searching for clues.

I stood some distance away from both groups, puffing a cigarette and trying to hide behind the smoke screen. A police breakdown truck was pulled up close to the edge and a rope from its winch dangled into the quarry like a fishing line. The rope moved from time to time and voices from the depths hollered: 'From me to you, Sid! . . . Down your end a bit! That's it, heave, heave! No, no, hold it there a minute! You've got the rope twisted! . . . Okay, let's try it once more. Gently does it, gently does it!' The copper in the cab of the truck activated the winch and, in fits and starts, Tomlinson was hoisted to the surface. The police always handle the dead a good deal more gently than they do the living.

When they'd got him up, and laid him out on the grass,

Professor Green-Parker knelt down and made a swift examination. I moved in a little closer and plugged into the famous pathologist's on-the-spot diagnosis of the cause of death.

'Uha uha, hmmm, uha uha,' said Green-Parker, examining first one area of the body and then another. 'Uha uha . . . how extraordinary . . . very interesting . . . uha uha.'

'Any notions?' asked Clews.

Green-Parker scratched his head thoughtfully for a moment, collecting his thoughts, then said: 'Extensive abrasions to the abdominal region, the thorax, pelvis and latissimus dorsi . . . The sternum is completely caved in, broken lumbar vertebrae, femur, metacarpus, also the scapula and the clavicle. . . . But I won't bore you with details.' He glanced up at the Superintendent and grinned. 'Looks very much as though you've got another murder on your hands, old boy.' He pointed a steady index finger at a large gash on Tomlinson's right arm. 'Nasty cut, but no blood. Same thing applies to the grazes and cuts elsewhere on the body. They were caused by the fall, of course, but he was dead before he went over.'

Clews showed no surprise.

'Another busted neck?' he asked.

''Fraid so,' said Green-Parker. 'Skilful blow to the cervical vertebra – probably a karate chop delivered with the right hand from behind. He didn't know what hit him.'

Clews raised an eyebrow.

'Same method as that used on the butler, what?' Sergeant du Ponte remarked.

I stared at him in amazement.

'I thought he was clobbered to death with a seven pound sledge hammer,' I said. 'It certainly looked like that.'

'You would,' sneered Clews. 'I would be grateful if you would keep your opinions to yourself.'

'Extensive damage was inflicted after death, what?' Algernon put in.

The image of a loose-fitting judo suit in the back of Pru's Lamborghini flashed blindingly across my mind's eye.

Clews glowered at Algernon.

'May I remind you, sergeant, that we do try not to pass on restricted information to suspects.'

83

Algernon did not enjoy being put down by his superior. He flushed and cast his eyes to the ground. I followed his gaze and saw what he saw, several feet away, half hidden by a clump of elephant grass. The sun glinted on it. We stepped forward a pace as one man to take a closer look; it glinted again. It looked very much like the barrel of a snub-nose handgun.

'Good heavens!' cried du Ponte, his voice trembling with excitement. 'What have we here?'

I kept shtoom.

'Unless my eyes deceive me, sir.' Algernon jumped up and down like an over-excited schoolgirl. 'That item on the ground over there, half hidden by that clump of elephant grass, is a fire-arm.'

Clews glanced in the direction in which the sergeant pointed. 'By george, du Ponte, I do believe you're right.'

Professor Green-Parker got up from where he'd been kneeling next to the body and the three men strode over to the clump of grass. I stood my ground.

'Stand back,' said Green-Parker and produced a pencil from the breast pocket of his Glenurquhart tweed hacking-jacket. 'This might be just the breakthrough we've been waiting for – especially if chummy has been accommodating enough to leave a nice set of prints on the butt.'

The pathologist pushed the pencil up the barrel and lifted the gun into the air.

I plunged my hands deep into my trouser pockets, sauntered over and craned my neck for a closer look. The weapon in the professor's hand was a .38 calibre Colt revolver. Something nasty happened in the pit of my stomach.

Clews leaned forward and sniffed the end of the barrel.

'Hasn't been fired recently,' he said.

'The firing pin is busted.' All heads turned in my direction.

'How do you know?' they chorused.

I shuffled my feet and mustered a boyish grin.

'It's my shooter.'

'Yours?' they chorused again.

I nodded.

A mean glint came into Clews' eye, but when he spoke his voice was calm and deceptively good natured.

84

'Care to tell us how it came to be here?' he asked.

'Tomlinson turned my gaff over yesterday and nicked it.' I glanced around the semi-circle of attentive faces. 'It's been a useful prop for threatening people with from time to time. The firing pin was already broken when I bought it off an old sweat in a pub nearly three years ago. I don't reckon it's spit lead since World War two.'

'What was the name of this man?' asked Clews.

'Sid.'

'Sid who?'

'I only met him the once and he never told me his other name.'

'Likely story, what.'

Clews gave me a long searching look.

'Doesn't seem very probable that Mr Tomlinson would break into your office with the sole purpose of stealing a gun with a broken firing pin, now does it?'

'Maybe he didn't know the firing pin was broken when he swiped it.'

'What else did he take?'

'Nothing.' My voice went into high-speed double-talk. 'I don't have the slightest idea why anyone would want to ransack my gaff. I don't own anything that would be of the slightest value to anyone, not even a second-hand junk dealer. I stayed the night with a lady friend and came back to the office just in time to catch Tomlinson near enough bang to rights. He got out of sight when he heard me coming, the next thing I know he's bouncing a dirty great blunt instrument off my nut. Maybe he did me with the butt of the shooter you have there. Why don't you check it out in the laboratory? If you find blood or mouse-coloured barnet, it's mine . . .'

'Who was the lady you were with last night?'

I smiled coyly and somehow managed to hold back the music-hall response.

'I don't think it would be fair on her to tell you,' I said.

Clews sighed.

'Sergeant du Ponte,' he said, 'would you kindly escort Mr Nelson back to the house. He will be coming back to the Yard with us.'

'What for?' I enquired dolefully. 'What for?'

The Superintendent glowered down at me from his full height for a long moment, then slowly lowered his head until his lips were close to my ear.

'You are beginning to get on my nerves, you little toe-rag,' he hissed. 'You are deeply implicated in this case, but I can assure you that you have obstructed my enquiries for the last time. Perhaps if I arrange for you to cool your heels in a nice little room with bars in the windows, for a week or two on remand, you will see the error of your ways and decide that a little cooperation with the police is no bad thing.'

It was the first time that I had ever seen Clews angry. Tempted though I certainly was to remonstrate with him about my legal rights, it struck me as unwise to provoke him into throwing the book at me. I stared up at him miserably, like a schoolboy who has just been admonished by the headmaster, and then set meekly off in the direction of the house with du Ponte in close attendance.

Sonia and Elinor were still pretty shaken by recent developments. They sat side by side on the drawing-room sofa with their backs straight and knees together like prim matrons taking tea at Fortnums. They followed me palely with their eyes as du Ponte escorted me to a nearby armchair. Neither spoke. I returned their gaze and tried to do something with my eyes that would indicate to them that they should keep it that way until they'd consulted the family lawyer. I couldn't tell whether they'd got the message.

When the scene-of-the crime investigations had been completed, Green-Parker accompanied the body to Silchester mortuary to carry out an autopsy and Clews put in an appearance in the drawing-room.

'Everything under control, sergeant?' he asked as he prowled through the door.

'Tickadyboo, sir,' said du Ponte.

Sonia, Elinor and I gazed at Clews in doleful silence – wondering which of us he was going to land on first. He chose Lady Sonia.

'I fully appreciate how upsetting all this must be for you, your

86

ladyship,' he said. 'But I wonder if you would mind answering one or two questions?'

Sonia bit her lower lip and gazed up at him mutely like a frightened child.

'Very well,' she replied at last in a very small voice. 'But there's nothing I can tell you.'

Du Ponte whipped out his notebook and waited expectantly, pencil poised.

'You may find that you know a great deal more than you realize, your ladyship.' Clews' voice was warm and creamy — the time-honoured police tactic of lulling a suspect into a sense of security. 'People often do.'

Sonia folded her hands in her lap and sighed.

'I have a memory like an absolute sieve.'

The sergeant made a note of it in his book.

'When was the last time you saw Mr Tomlinson alive?' Clews asked politely.

'This morning,' replied Sonia nervously. 'No, yesterday morning, or was it last night?' She gave Elinor an appealing glance. 'When was it? I really can't remember.'

'Think,' said Clews.

'The day before yesterday. That's right. He was going up to town, I think. He went off after tea and I haven't seen him since.'

'Was this house Mr Tomlinson's fixed abode?' du Ponte put in.

'I don't know what you mean.'

'He lived here, what?'

Sonia got up and walked over to the fireplace, fumbled a filter-tipped cigarette from a silver box on the mantelpiece and lit it with a chunky table lighter. She blew a cloud of smoke into the air and faced Clews.

'Patrick was an old and valued friend of the family.' She appeared to have regained her composure and addressed the superintendent in the sharp, disdainful tone that the aristocracy reserve for those they regard as socially inferior. Which is more or less everybody.

'Of course, he was most welcome to stay at Bramley Hall as often, and for as long, as he wished. But it would be quite wrong to infer from that that this was a permanent residence. When he was in London he stayed at his club, I believe. His family home in Lincolnshire has been let for some time.'

'Which club was that exactly?' asked Clews.

Lady Sonia brushed a loose strand of hair from her face with the back of her hand, and stuck her nose in the air.

'He belonged to Boodles, the Beef Steak and the Rag – but he usually stayed at Boodles.'

'He didn't stay at the Peveril residence in Belgravia?'

'Occasionally.' She gave Clews a withering stare. 'It is quite a large house and there is always plenty of room to put up one's friends.'

'You say that the day before yesterday was the last time you saw him alive. Are you certain about that?'

'Absolutely,' Sonia affirmed in a high pitched staccato. 'He was the finest man I've ever known – so kind and considerate. God only knows what I would have done without his support while my husband was carrying on his sordid little affair with that slut in London.'

Clews' interest quickened.

'Affair?'

'That's what I said,' she snapped. 'He has been seeing her for some time now. Of course, he thought I didn't know a thing about it. Men always do. But I knew all right, right from the very first day.'

I sank into my chair.

'Who is she?' asked Clews.

Lady Sonia pointed a long slender finger in my direction.

'Why don't you ask him?' she said.

'Me?' I gulped.

'Yes you! She's your client isn't she?'

Clews stood four-square before me. His head seemed to brush the ceiling. I glanced up at him through my fingers and cringed even further into the chair.

'Is this true?' he demanded. 'What's her name?'

The jig was well and truly up and there seemed nothing for it, except come my guts.

'Her name is Prudence Pride,' I said. 'She hired me to find Sir Samford and I sincerely wish she hadn't. This case has caused

88

me nothing but aggravation right from the beginning. People keep on trying to kill me . . .'

'That's nothing to the trouble you're going to get from me if you continue to suppress important evidence,' interrupted Clews.

'He knows plenty,' blazed Sonia. 'He's been following Patrick and me all over the place for the past few weeks – spying on us. Of course he thought he was *so* clever, but Patrick noticed him right from the first. Go on, Superintendent, ask him about my husband's mistress. He knows all about her – I wouldn't be surprised if that little slut isn't hiding Samford at this very moment.' She burst into floods of hysterical tears and fell back onto the sofa.

I took a deep breath: 'Look, the thing is, Super, I haven't really been trying to pull the wool over your mince pies. It's just that I haven't really had all that much hard evidence to share with you. Miss Pride is my client, but she had nothing to do with the Parkhurst murder or Sir Samford's disappearance – and it is my professional duty to protect her, after all. If a private enquiry agent goes around gossiping about his clients he soon won't have any.'

'Cut the moody, Ed,' snapped Clews. 'Get on with it, I want times, names and places.'

'Give us a chance,' I said and then, with lights and shades, oos and arrs from the ladies and grunts from the cops, I related my side of it to the assembled company.

There were a few omissions, of course, I didn't mention Pru's weekly tuition in the martial arts or the little hideaway in the mountains above Monte Carlo. And I also stayed shtoom about bumping into Pru at the scene of the original crime.

'That it?' asked Clews when I'd finished.

'Yes.'

'You're sure?'

'Sure, I'm sure.'

'Nothing to add?'

'Like what?'

'Well, do you by any chance know where the jewels are now?'

'Tomlinson knocked them off, like I said, and I haven't seen them since.'

'He's lying,' choked Sonia. 'Patrick would never have done such a thing.'

I shrugged and fumbled in my jacket pocket for cigarettes.

'My theory, for what it's worth,' I volunteered, 'is that someone, maybe Sir Samford and maybe someone else, has got it in for this family. It may have something to do with the sparklers and it may not. My guess is that it goes deeper than that, a lot deeper.'

Clews gave me the kind of withering look that no one likes to get from a policeman.

'Outside, you.' He jerked a thumb over his shoulder. 'Go and wait in my car.'

'What for?' I bleated. 'I've told you everything I know.'

'I want it in writing,' he rapped. 'You going quietly or in handcuffs?'

CHAPTER SEVENTEEN

Clews and du Ponte joined me in the black police Wolseley in their own good time. Constable Coldingley let in the clutch and accelerated smoothly away from the house.

I was sitting in the front with the driver and caught a glimpse of one or two things that were lost on the Super in the back. Half way down the drive a bulky tearaway was weeding a flower bed – and it wasn't Elinor's right hand man, Mr Tidmarsh. At the gate another villainous-looking character was sniffing a rose in the hedgerow and half a mile down the road, two more were having a quiet smoke in a big Yankee motor parked in a lay-by. It was a car that I seemed to recall seeing before.

Wherever I moved in this case, I seemed to see the kind of faces that one would normally associate with wanted posters. In the sunlit greenery of the summer countryside they stuck out like sore thumbs.

It was a strain not to deduce that the underworld were involved in the affair somewhere along the line – but quite where had me baffled. Were they after the jewels? Out to revenge the brutal murder of Gloria's older brother? In the pay of the blackmailer, Patrick Tomlinson, or were they hanging around in the hope of collecting some of Samford's outstanding gambling debts? It even crossed my mind that this was the 'protection' that Pru had mysteriously promised me.

I bent my brain to the puzzle and tried to come up with the murderer of Parkhurst and Tomlinson – none of my business of course, not being the kind of chump who undertook murder investigations. I found that, without over-reaching my mental limitations, I could make out a pretty convincing case against any of them – Samford, Pru, Sonia, Elinor and the unknown James. And Willy Paradis knew a lot more about it than he was letting on, as well.

From Bramley Hall to Scotland Yard, at high speed, took us exactly fifty-seven minutes, door to door.

On this occasion Clews did not invite me into his office for a cosy chat. He ordered du Ponte to conduct me to a sparsely furnished room, as though I was a common criminal.

'Any chance of a cuppa tea?' I asked, as I slumped into a hard wooden chair behind a plain white wood table. 'My throat's parched.'

Algernon gave me a look that left little room for interpretation – he was very far from pleased with me.

'No,' he said.

'Why not?'

'You've upset the chief and when someone upsets the chief it's beastly for everyone, what?'

I thumped the table with a clenched fist. 'Listen, you. I want some tea or my lawyer, take your pick.'

Further argument was averted by the arrival of Clews. He brushed past Algernon and plonked himself down in a chair opposite me. Our eyes locked.

'I want some tea,' I told him.

The Superintendent glanced over his shoulder.

'Two teas please, sergeant, if you would be so kind.' His voice was as sweet as molasses but full of hidden menace.

Du Ponte glared at me for an instant, then flung out of the room and slammed the door behind him.

'What's up with him?' I asked.

Clews eyed me across the table.

'I think you've rubbed him up the wrong way. The sergeant tends to get rather touchy when little worms like you try to mess him about.'

'Now don't start all that again,' I cried. 'How many times do I have to tell you that I don't know any more than I've already told you?'

'Depends.'

'On what?'

'How long it takes before I believe you.'

'In that case we're going to be here all night.'

'That,' Clews agreed, 'is a distinct possibility.'

Du Ponte returned with the tea in the fullness of time. Mine was cold, without sugar. I sipped it with distaste but didn't complain.

Clews rested his elbow on the table and his chin on a clenched fist.

'Now then, Ed,' he began, 'what I'd like you to do is cast your mind back to the Parkhurst murder.'

'The Parkhurst murder,' I repeated.

'Yes, you know, the butler whose battered body you stumbled upon in the Peveril's Belgravia residence?'

'Yes, yes. What about it?'

'I want you to cast your mind back to it.'

'I am, I am.'

The superintendent smiled at the sergeant; the sergeant smiled back.

'Now we're getting somewhere,' said Clews.

'Where are we getting?' I demanded. 'Look, I'm getting a bit sick of this game. Let's play something else.'

'Good idea,' cried Algernon. 'Let's play "kick the uncooperative witness around the interview room," what?'

I gave him a watery smile and turned to Clews.

'Why don't you simply ask me whatever it is you want to know?'

'Who else was there?' he asked.

'Who else was where?'

He sighed wearily.

92

'I thought you said you'd cast your mind back to the Parkhurst murder?'

'I have, I have,' I assured him. 'Like I already told you, I saw no one.'

It is extremely bad form for a man to finger a girl he's shared a bed with. But Pru was downright dangerous to know and a lot of the fun had gone out of covering for her.

Clews smiled at me across the table. The smile had no humour in it.

'Tell me again?' he said.

'I know my rights. Either you charge me with something or I'm going home.'

A pained expression passed over the Superintendent's face.

'Are you refusing to help us with our enquiries?'

'How can I help you? Sometimes I can't even tie my own shoelaces.'

'You don't make things very easy for yourself, do you?'

I made as if to get up from the table.

Algernon laid a heavy hand on my shoulder and said: 'Sit down, there's a good fellow.'

The grilling went on for hours.

How did I first become involved in the case? How much money did Prudence Pride pay me? Why didn't I bring the jewels straight to the police when I found them in the bust of Shelley? Did I have a firearms licence for my gun?

'Why not, don't you know that it's against the law to carry a gun without a licence even if the firing pin is broken?'

'How would you like five years in the nick for hampering police investigations?'

'Where is Sir Samford Peveril?'

'How do we know if you're telling the truth?'

'How would you like a sock on the jaw, what?'

The questions came thick and fast, first from Clews, then from du Ponte and then from Clews again. When, in the early hours of the morning, they eventually let up we all had our jackets off and our shirts were sticking to our bodies with sweat. I'd held my end up, but like everything else, I had to do it the hard way.

Without telling me what was going to happen next,

Superintendent Clews leapt to his feet and stalked out of the room with du Ponte on his heels. I guessed that the 'd gone out into the corridor to cook up their next move. I stood up and took a turn around the unpleasant little room in an effort to get the blood circulating in my legs. I'd been sitting so long I feared that I might have to walk sideways for the rest of my life. I also had a headache, my buttocks were sore and I'd run out of cigarettes. A pimply young constable came in and stood sentinel by the door.

'Got any fags on you, mate?' I asked.

He gazed blankly at the cream-coloured wall and said nothing.

The superintendent and his sergeant returned when they were good and ready. They looked far from happy.

'All right, Nelson,' grunted Clews, 'you can go.'

'Mr Nelson to you,' I grunted right back at him. 'It's about time.'

Both men looked daggers at me.

'Don't push your luck, sonny,' warned Clews. 'Go on, get out of my sight.'

I took heed of his warning and made a swift departure.

Tangerine had cleaned the place up a treat. There wasn't much she could do about the busted furniture, but she'd certainly been busy with the broom and duster. The most moving touch was the pretty square of flowered damask with which she had patched the horse hair sofa. She'd left me a sweet little message on the desk pad, it read: 'What a dangerous sex life you do lead, ducky. You owe me a fiver for the char-ing. Don't get killed before you pay me. Love, T.'

What had gone wrong at the Post Office I did not know, but the telephone engineers had been round and re-connected my only link with the outside world. Could it be that the age of miracles had not passed?

The lock was broken where Tomlinson had jemmied the door. I hooked a chair under it before I crumpled onto the sofa.

CHAPTER EIGHTEEN

How long I'd been asleep before I was brutally awakened by the phone going off like a burglar alarm, I do not know. It certainly hadn't been for long enough. I fumbled the receiver off the hook, put it to my ear and Diamonds Silverman said: 'Zatchew, Ed?'

'It's me,' I groaned.

'Yuh vorkin' for Mizz Pride, right?'

'Right.'

'Vell, yuh know dem gems votcha bin carryin' on alarmin' abaht?'

'What about them?'

'I've got 'em.'

That jerked me out of the infinite weariness with which I had conducted my end of the conversation thus far – I was suddenly wide awake.

'The Peveril sparklers?' I queried in disbelief.

'Dems de vones yuh bin tryin' t'lay yuh mitts on, ain't dey?'

'You said it,' I cried. 'How the hell did you come by them?'

'Yuh do a big tavour by me if yuh don't arst such a question,' Diamonds replied reprovingly. 'I make a meet mitchew at de 'Ide Away six o'clock t'night – ve do a bitta biziness, maybe.'

'I'll be there,' I said, but he'd already hung up and I was talking to the dialling tone. Then came a clunk-click. The boys were at it again.

I glanced at my wrist – no watch. I was in the market for a bent time-piece that had fallen, not too heavily, off the back of a lorry. I dialled 123 and a recorded female voice told me flatly that at the third stroke it would be four-twenty and ten seconds.

'Morning or afternoon?' I said, in the absence of a more polished witticism and went back to sleep. I awoke with a jolt half an hour later in a river of sweat; I'd had another rotten dream.

I washed and shaved at the corner sink and put on clean clothes from the skin out. Then I made some instant coffee – I'd've preferred tea but Tomlinson had smashed my nice old brown teapot in a fit of pique – lit a cigarette and sat down at my desk.

I'd sipped half the coffee and smoked half the cigarette when the phone rang again. It was Lady Sonia.

'Mr Nelson?' She sounded irritated.

I said 'Speaking'.

'Your car is standing in my drive and I have no wish for it to remain there for a moment longer than is absolutely necessary. I would be grateful, therefore, if you would have the courtesy to remove it forthwith.' It sounded like she was reading a solicitor's letter.

'Easier said than done, m'lady,' I replied agreeably. 'Trouble is I happen to be in London.'

'I am well aware of that, Mr Nelson. I had the greatest difficulty in obtaining your telephone number. When may I expect you?'

' 'Fraid I can't come right away . . .'

She blew her top. Her voice became shrill and stabbed at me along the telephone wire.

'I'm not having your beastly car blocking my drive. Not having it, do you hear? I'll have it dragged away to the nearest scrap yard . . .'

'Control yourself, you silly woman,' I barked. And to my complete surprise, her shrills petered out in a sob.

'Now I come to think of it, I hired that car locally. I'll ring the garage and get them to pick it up right away,' I promised.

'Oh . . . thank you,' she choked, and made no little effort to get a hold on herself. 'I'm sorry to have shouted at you. I suppose I'm terribly overwrought.'

'Of course, you've been through a lot.'

'It's all so frightening and . . . unspeakably awful.'

'You can say that again.' I wished that I didn't have such a pronouced flair for saying the wrong things.

'Patrick's funeral is on Thursday,' she went on. 'The undertaker couldn't arrange anything before then. Three people have died of old age in the village this week,' she added by way of explanation for the delay.

'Comes to us all sooner or later.'

'Mr Nelson?'

'Yes.'

'Would you care to come to the funeral?'

'Not much.'

'Oh please do,' she pleaded. 'You may discover something to your advantage.'

I wondered what she meant by that, but decided not to ask.

'Well, I er . . .'

'Do please come. There are so many things that I'd like to explain to you.' Her voice was growing more strident. 'Not to mince matters, Mr Nelson, I'd like your professional advice.'

'I'm not working on the murders. That's police business.'

'I know. You're looking for my husband, aren't you?'

I wasn't enjoying our conversation very much. After a testy start, her ladyship was now actually cooing and pleading and getting on my wick. But I wasn't going to let her off that lightly.

'As a matter of fact,' I said, 'there are one or two odds and ends you might be able to clear up for me. For example, I'd be fascinated to know how you came to have sand on your shoes when you returned from your lunch with the rural dean in Silchester?'

'Sand?'

'You know, the stuff they make whisky tumblers out of. There was a quantity of it on your shoes and it looked like the same kind of sand I saw at the edge of the slate quarry.'

She had no pat answer to that, and didn't offer one.

'The funeral will be at two o'clock sharp on Thursday afternoon — I will expect to see you then,' she commanded and hung up. There was a whirr, then the familiar clicking noise on the line.

I snarled like a thirties movie gangster: 'Leave off tapping my blower, yuh lousy creeps!'

CHAPTER NINETEEN

Len Stokes, the pouchy-faced minder, said: 'Wotcha, cock,' as I strolled into the Hide Away and I said: 'Wotcha, cock,' right back at him.

He was studying the racing results in the stop press of the evening paper.

'Done any good?' I asked.

He gave me that weary, crestfallen look that inveterate gamblers have in common with whipped dogs.

'Got cattled by a rank outsider in the 4.30 at Epsom,' he informed me. ' 'Ad a jacks each way on Fleet Foot, stone bonkin' certainty it was s'posed to be. Right shtoomer it turned out to be – came soddin' nowhere. Bloody animal was got at by one of them dope gangs, I reckon – diabolical liberty is wot I call it.'

'Never mind,' I chortled. 'You must be lucky in love.'

Len was not a good loser.

'Wotcha larffin' at?' he snarled.

'Nothing.'

'Well, pack it in then or I'll be forced to fill yuh in.'

I wiped the grin off my face and made my way to the bar.

I was twenty minutes early for my meeting with Diamonds – ample time to get in a couple of large Hankey Bannisters. I climbed aboard a bar stool, lit a cigarette and caught the eye of the bartender. As he poured my drink I glanced surreptitiously about to see who was there. If the phone tappers had blown down their employer's earhole about my appointment with Diamonds, it was likely that other interested parties would put in an appearance.

Out of the corner of my eye, in the mirrored bottle shelves behind the bar, I caught a glimpse of something that shook me rigid. The thing I saw was a darkly beautiful girl, dressed to kill in a glistening gold polyester lamé siren suit, with Fiorucci boots to match. She looked remarkably like Prudence Pride.

She was seated at a secluded corner table in deep conclave with Willy Paradis. My view of them was partly obscured by a clutch of punters around the roulette wheel. But when they bowed their heads to place bets on the green baize I got a clear view of the table, and after two spins I was no longer in the slightest doubt.

I swallowed the first drink whole and with the second clutched tightly in my fist, I slid off the bar stool, sauntered over to the roulette wheel and mingled with the punters.

Willy and Pru had their heads close together, and were deep in whispered conversation. From the way they were rabbiting you'd've said they knew each other intimately. Even if, like one

98

or two other feather-minded upper-class birds of my acquaintance, she was looking for something with menace, I couldn't help feeling that Willy was a little old for her.

I loitered by the roulette table for several minutes, turning this amazing discovery over in my mind and wondering what my next move should be. There were grave risks involved in fronting them up, particularly if Willy lost his temper and called upon Len to give me a bit of a tuning up. But curiosity impelled me to investigate – just as soon as I'd finished my drink and maybe a half dozen more to give me Dutch courage.

The little white ball came to rest on twenty-seven red; I glanced idly down at the table – nobody had any chips on it. When I looked up Pru was staring at me. Our eyes locked for an eternity and her mouth formed a perfect O. Then she turned and whispered something to Willy.

If my legs hadn't turned to jelly I'd've made a run for it. Willy raised a hand and beckoned to me. I glanced at the punters on either side of me, then pointed at my chest and mouthed: 'Who, me?' Willy nodded gravely and I slowly tottered around the table, edging between the gamblers.

Half way round I trod on a pound chip that had fallen to the floor. I stooped down, furtively scooped it up and tossed it onto the table. It rolled across the green baize and came to rest on thirteen black.

'Bit early for yer appointment, ain'tcha, Ed?' remarked Willy when I joined them.

I shrugged agreement and slumped into a vacant chair. There was no longer any mystery about who was having my blower tapped.

Willy said: 'Fancy a drop of bubbly?'

I raised an eyebrow: 'We celebrating something?'

His upper lips curved over his teeth in an ugly smile. 'Yuh don't need no reason to push the boat out when yuh can play the dirty games of this dirty society and come out on top.' Willy was quite the philosopher when he put his mind to it.

He snapped his fingers at a passing waitress and she brought another glass. Pru wrenched the bottle out of the ice bucket and did the honours with the Dom Perignon.

''Ere's to crime!' toasted Willy and grinned hugely.

99

I raised my glass to him.

'Cheers,' I said and swigged the bubbly as though it was whisky.

Pru balanced her champagne glass between a dainty forefinger and thumb and gave me that special look that girls give boys they've been to bed with.

'Do stop looking so suspicious, love,' she sighed. 'There's no big mystery.'

I didn't quite agree, but I held back the baited questions that I was bursting to unload.

'*Treize, noir!*' hollered the cockney croupier at the roulette wheel. The punters glanced enquiringly at one another.

'*Treize,* bleedin' *noir!*' He banged his rake on the table.

'Thirteen, black – whose is it? Look lively, I ain't got all soddin' day.'

I leapt to my feet and dashed across the room shouting: 'It's mine, it's mine!'

The croupier leered at me ominously and pushed my winnings across the green baize.

'This ain't a tombola at a poxy vicarage tea party,' he exhaled angrily. 'If yuh gonna 'ave a bet, 'ave a bet an' don't go for a walk between spins.'

I scooped up the chips and poured them into my jacket pocket.

'Thanks for the good advice,' I said.

Pru and Willy were enjoying a private joke when I got back. I wondered if it was at my expense.

'Wot time did Diamonds say 'e was gonna show up?' Willy asked.

I glanced at the electric wall clock.

'He's late. He said six.'

'Did he mention *how* he came by the jewels?' asked Pru earnestly.

I gave her a slow penetrating look.

'Did I say he had the jewels?' She tried out a winsome smile. It was not a success and I passed on hurriedly, without waiting for her answer. 'If you're thinking that he bumped off Patrick and swiped the sparklers, your guess is as good as mine – I take it that you are aware that Tomlinson's been murdered.'

100

'My boys were down there,' Willy said flatly.

Pru moistened her lower lip, gave me a frightened little look and said nothing.

'Listen, baby,' said Willy, coming to her aid, 'yuh ain't gotta fing in the world to worry about.' His lips tightened and a hard glint came into his eyes. 'Leave Diamonds to me.'

I didn't like the way he said that at all and resolved to warn Diamonds as soon as I could. Meanwhile it seemed like a good idea to change from one dangerous topic to another dangerous topic.

'Listen,' I blurted out. 'I don't want to get personal or anything. But how come you two know each other?'

Willy looked at Pru. She looked back at him and smiled faintly; then they both looked at me.

'If I tell yuh the full strengff,' Willy said stiffly. ''Ave I yuh word that it don't go no furvver?'

I nodded vigorously.

'You have it.'

He glanced about to be sure that we were not being overheard.

'Prudence is my daughter,' he declared.

I let out an involuntary yelp of laughter and clapped a hand over my mouth.

He went on soberly: ''Er mum was Angie O' 'Agan.'

'Not Angie O'Hagan, the daughter of Machine-Gun Jack O'Hagan, who used to have the Silk Cockatoo before the war?' I enquired excitedly.

Willy beamed with delight, obviously pleased that she was still remembered.

'Angie 'ad a smashin' voice and she used to sing at the Silk Cockatoo; great draw in 'er days she was – that's where I met 'er. First time I seen 'er she 'ad on a green evenin' frock an' ostrich feavvers in 'er barnet. She was up on stage beltin' out the latest 'it, an Al Jolson number called: '*Where Did Robinson Crusoe Take Friday on Saturday Night?*' I fink it was. Any old 'ow, me an' Angie took a shine to each uvver right off and started goin' steady.' He hesitated and gazed into the middle distance with the eyes of one who had seen too much and forgotten too little. Then he smiled wistfully, as though recalling

101

a distant and pleasurable memory and said: 'I was on Spats DeGrazio's firm in them days – Spats and Machine-gun was deadly rivals and never left off 'avin' the needle to each uvver – so me an' Angie 'ad to do oûr courtin' on the sly. But in the death we wound up gettin' 'itched one Saturday mornin' down Stepney Green registry orffice, then we scarpered across the Irish Sea to a little village in Galway for our 'oneymoon. Angie was born there so we didn't 'ave no bovva layin' low. Then the next fing we know, it's all over the linens that the feud between Spats and Machine-Gun 'as 'otted up a bit and they wind up bumpin' each uvver off in a shoot-out down the Mile End Road. Spats plugged Machine-Gun Jack froo the strawberry tart wiv 'is 45 and Machine-Gun sprayed Spats as 'e went down. It come out later that Machine-Gun Jack 'ad already kicked the bucket when 'e pulled the trigger – sortta nervous reaction yuh might call it – but they took twenty eight slugs out of Spats, about of pound of lead if I remember rightly.' His voice petered out and his eyes dimmed. 'Angie was pretty cut up about 'er daddy gettin' rubbed out, even if 'e did go out spittin' lead, and she swore on a stack of Bibles that she'd never set foot on this side of the water again as long as she lived.'

He gave Pru an affectionate pat on the cheek and his face lit up in a paternal smile. 'My little girl was born and bred over there, same as her muvver. I was double sure she weren't gonna get mixed up in the rackets. Every bent penny that came my way went to make sure of that. She went to all the best schools and, so's she wouldn't get connected with me business empire, she ain't even got me name – I 'ad a grey'ound in them days called Cockney Pride and that's where 'er surname come from. In the death she got finished off in Switzerland, then I dropped a few 'undred in the right places and launched 'er in 'igh society, like a deb. Ain't no one in this world good enough for 'er, but I'm gonna make double sure the bloke she ends up wiv is a Duke or a Earl, or the worst way a Lord.'

Willy, like most tearaways was a right-wing reactionary.

'Sir Samford good enough for you?' I asked.

'No one ain't good enough for 'er, like I said.' He smiled at Pru. 'But if my little girl wants 'im she can 'ave 'im.'

Pru smiled back at him.

'When I'm sure, you'll be the first to know, Dad,' she said.

'Yuh don't 've to worry about a fing, so long as I'm around,' said Willy. 'Readies nor anyfing . . .'

'Money is not the problem just now,' she reminded him.

'Don't trouble yer pretty little 'ead.' He eyed me coldly. 'My boys've got a lead on Samford's whereabouts. I'll 'ave 'im back for yuh in a couple of days. If it comes out that 'e did 'is butler in, I'll fix it so's yuh can live 'appily ever after in Brazil or some uvver place that ain't got no extradition agreement wiv the Yard.'

Pru didn't look as pleased as I'd expected. She glanced at her wrist watch, then looked towards the door.

'Where on earth can Diamonds be?' she asked. 'He's almost an hour late.'

I did what I could to hide my irritation.

'I suppose you just happened to be in the neighbourhood and thought it might be fun to share my date with him, did you?'

Willy focused his animosity on me, it was never far from the surface.

'Watch yuh lip, loser.'

'It's alright, Dad,' Pru said easily. 'You might as well know, Ed. I once set it up for Diamonds to steal the Peveril jewels myself. Sammy couldn't flog them because they were part of the family trust I told you about. So Diamonds said he would oblige.'

' 'E sent Tools Gunstone out to do the job,' Willy put in. 'And that butler geezer captured 'im bang to rights just as 'e climbed in the burnt . . . Now the latest is Diamonds says 'e's got 'em.' He flicked his eyes on me again. 'Now it wouldn't be all that favourite of ole Diamonds to pull a double cross on 'is own mates – would it?'

'It would not be *favourite*,' I agreed and scraped back my chair.

'Are you going?' asked Pru.

'Don't see what there is to hang about here for,' I said. 'Diamonds isn't going to show up now and I don't expect you'll be needing my services from now on?'

She gave me a level appraising look:

'You are quite wrong, Ed. It was Daddy's idea that you could

103

keep an eye on Sonia and Patrick without anyone suspecting us. You've been marvellous. And she's asked you to Patrick's funeral, hasn't she?'

I nodded glumly.

'In that case,' she went on hurriedly, as I got to my feet. 'You might like to let us know how it goes off.'

'Just keep an eye on 'er, Ed,' advised Willy.

Pru whispered: 'Don't hate me.'

'Never hate my clients,' I said.

She seemed pleased to hear that.

'Be in touch?' she asked warmly.

I gave her a curt nod and pushed and apologized my way blindly to the bar. Fifteen minutes snailed by and Diamonds still hadn't shown up. I ordered a double Hankey Bannister's for the road, gulped it down in one go, then did some more pushing and apologizing to the bullet-proof cashier's window and converted my chips into readies. Thirty-three quid is not the kind of money to be sneezed at even if the pound is sick from inflation.

CHAPTER TWENTY

I awoke next morning with a jolt. Waking up in the morning with a jolt was getting to be a habit I could've easily done without. There were gruff voices outside on the landing.

'... No, no not that way yuh burk ... around to the right a bit ... The right, that's the bleedin' left. . . . It ain't my fault, I can't get it up, mate. It's too soddin' big.'

I pulled on my trousers and padded barefoot across the room. I paused at the door, zipped up my fly, gently turned the handle and sneaked a peek. Black Satin Hotpants was escorting two burly workmen up the stairs. The men were carrying a pink Slumberland, posture-sprung, double divan bed.

'Hi neighbour!' cried Hotpants. 'How's the head?'

'Splitting and not likely to get any better with all this racket going on.'

My sudden appearance gave the men an excuse to take a

104

breather. They dropped the bed and glared at me. A blue slip of paper fluttered to the floor and, without thinking, I stooped down and picked it up.

'It ain't our fault mate,' grunted the heavier of the two. 'There oughta be a extra charge for delivering fings wot don't fit in the lift.'

The other took a half-smoked cigarette from behind his ear, stuck it into the corner of his mouth and set light to it with a safety match.

'You're dead right there, Bert,' he agreed.

Hotpants gave me a cheeky wink then, hands resting lightly on her hips and an enticing glint in her eye, she turned to the men.

'Aw, cummon fellers, don't be like that! Two he-men like you shouldn't have any trouble carrying a bed up a couple of flights of stairs.' She squeezed the bicep of the bigger man and giggled. 'Ooo, you're so *strong* – I'll just bet you look sensational without any clothes on.'

They didn't need asking twice, they grabbed the bed and wrestled it up the stairs.

'Mind if I come in for a minute?' she asked and brushed by me without waiting for a reply.

'So you got the vacancy?' I said, nodding towards the ceiling.

She dangled a naked leg over the edge of the sofa.

'That's right, passion.'

'How did you persuade the agent to let you have it?' I asked. 'He's a flint-hearted, tight-fisted, property tycoon and his leases are liable to have more clauses than a Dalmatian has spots.'

She laughed.

'He's not queer though.' She twisted her head and gave me another of her winks. 'If a geezer isn't queer, there's nothing a girl can't get out of him if she puts her mind to it – sometimes even if he is.'

There wasn't much I could say to that, so I just smiled half-heartedly. She bounced off the sofa and made for the door.

'Fancy christening the new bed?'

'Yes of course,' I said. 'But not right now.'

'Why not? You can have it for nothing.'

'Can't stand the guilt.'

'Silly boy.' She opened the door. 'Maybe some other time when the bed's been broken in a bit.'

I slumped down at the desk and found that I still had the slip of paper in my hand that I'd picked up outside. It was an invoice from John Lewis for one pink Slumberland, posture-sprung, double divan bed. Then my blood froze. The invoice was made out to Mr Patrick Tomlinson.

When I'd washed, shaved and dressed I settled down at my desk, with a cup of Nescafé and a cigarette, and pondered my next move. The quaggy spot I was in was getting stickier and stickier by the minute. My delectable client had turned out to be the daughter of a bad man from the underworld. The brass upstairs was in the pay of a deceased blackmailer. The blackmailer's moll had cordially invited me to his funeral. And Clews had made it blindingly obvious that he considered me to be a bigger liar than Tom Pepper; and he's hot. All things considered my present position left a great deal to be desired – particularly for an all round sweet lad who didn't handle murder cases.

My ponderings were interrupted by a light tap on the door.

'It's no good you trying to get me to change my mind!' I shouted. 'I don't want to go to bed with you now or later, even if you're handing out Green Shield stamps.'

The door opened and Diamonds Silverman waddled in.

'So is dat a nice way to talk?' he asked. 'Votcha take me for, a poofter or sumtink?'

'Sorry, Diamonds, I thought you were the scrubber who's moved in upstairs,' I apologized. 'Come in and take a pew.'

He crossed the room and sat down on the edge of the sofa.

'You want some instant coffee?' I asked. 'I haven't got any tea.'

'Is instant coffee kosha?'

'How should I know?'

'In dat case I don't vont to risk it.' He glanced around the office, sniffed disdainfully and said: 'Looks like yuh got on de wrong side of de Borough Council demolition gang.' He laughed heartily at his own joke.

I waited for him to quieten down, then changed the subject.

'How comes you stood me up last night?'

'I voz ready to keep de appointment I make mitchew.' He

106

threw his hands in the air and addressed the heavens. 'So vot 'appens? I tell yuh vot 'appens – Gloria she come on de blower an' say I gotta baby-sit mit 'er French poodle on account of it ain't feelin' vell an' she can't take it to de strip joint mit 'er like usual – dat's vot 'appened. My life, if Gloria Randy says I gotta take care of de mutt den I takes care of de mutt, or she say nasty tings to me like she don't love me no more, already.'

Personally, I thought he'd been steering clear of Willy. But if he preferred to put it in that romantic and touching way, it was no skin off my nose.

Enough time having been spent on pleasantries, I got down to cases.

'You reckoned you've got the Peveril gems?'

'I got 'em,' he replied cagily.

'Can I take a butchers at them?'

'Not so fast, kiddo.' A shrewd glint came into his eye. 'First I vont to know 'ow much de insurance company vill give for de pleasure of deir return?'

'Ten per cent. You know that's the going rate as well as I do.'

Diamonds shrivelled.

'So it's a crime to arst?'

'Quit stalling,' I rasped. 'Let's see them.'

He slipped a podgy hand into the pocket of his thick Crombie overcoat.

'Such impatience,' he grumbled. 'A goy don't know nutting about de art of makin' a business deal . . .' He tossed a small black velvet bag onto the desk. 'Rush, rush, 'urry, 'urry! Goys know nutting else.'

I grabbed the bag, fumbled with the silk tape at the opening and emptied the contents onto the ink blotter. The goodies that spilled out looked as hot as hell. There were diamond and sapphire rings, a couple of ropes of pearls, several sets of emerald and ruby ear-pendants, two or three jewel-encrusted bracelets and a truly magnificent sapphire, diamond and ruby necklace that was worth more money than was likely to pass through my hands even if business improved ten-fold and I lived to be a hundred and twenty-eight.

'Votchew tink?' Diamonds asked excitedly. 'Did yuh ever see such 'igh quality merchandise?'

107

I inspected first one piece, then another and finally sat back in my chair.

'Finest collection of sparklers I've ever clapped eyes on,' I conceded. 'Pity it isn't the right stuff.'

'Votchew mean it an't de right stuff?' he hollered.

I picked up the necklace and caressed it lovingly.

'High quality merchandise, like you say. But someone's been taking you on . . . They are definitely not the Peveril jewels.'

Diamonds exhaled a guttural laugh.

'Not de Peveril gems, not de Peveril gems!' he cried scornfully.

'I put de vord about I'm interested in de Peveril haul an' from de most reliable source dey come. Dey burn a big enough 'ole in my pocket to be nutting else but de Peveril gems. But now yuh say I've been conned.'

'They're certainly hot enough to be the Peveril jewels,' I interrupted him. 'Someone is bound to be searching for them high and low, but not the Peveril family.'

Diamonds thought it over for a moment.

'I tink I 'ave a sneakin' sus where dey come from if dey're not de Peverel tom.' He looked me straight in the eyes. 'But 'ow yuh know a Peveril gem ven yuh see it?'

It was a reasonable enquiry. I mulled it over and decided that it could do no real harm to tell him.

I said: 'I had them until a day or two ago.'

'Do me a tavour,' Diamonds chuckled. 'Yuh make a little joke, right?'

'Wrong,' I said. 'I had them until an upper-class twit tapped me on the sconce and lifted them. The upper-class twit has got himself murdered but the tom is still on the missing list.'

'So 'ow comes yuh arst me to get 'em, ven yuh got 'em already?'

'Didn't have them then.' I gazed regretfully at the array of sparklers on the ink blotter. 'Like I say, all we've got to do is wait 'til the scream goes up for this little lot. Then return them to a grateful insurance company.'

Diamonds swept the gems into a pile and scooped them into the bag.

'Dere vill be no scream for dis liddle lot, I tink. Dey come from de strong boxes in dat Mayfair bank vot got done last veek.' He spoke with measured certainty. 'De law says dey don't know a ting about vot's missin' on account of rich people are liable to keep tings in strong boxes dey don't vont de taxesman to know about.'

Diamonds got up to leave.

'Hold on a minute,' I said. 'I'm in the market for a watch.'

A slightly depressed expression hardened the lines of Diamonds' face. Then suddenly he shouted with laughter.

'I offer yuh enough tomfoolery to ransom de entire crowned 'eads of Europe an' all yuh can say is yuh vont to buy a votch – yuh take me for a Oxford Street *schlepper*, already?'

I smiled broadly.

'I need a watch,' I told him slowly, 'because I busted mine on Tools Gunstone's kisser. I know that Tools runs little errands for you from time to time and it just so happens that he was paying a social call on a certain party without an invitation, which is how come I busted my watch on his kisser.

'What's more, Willy Paradis is keen to know if you had a hand in the demise of the upper-class twit who nicked the jewels off me. One thing can lead to another, you know, and he's not best pleased with your interest in the Peveril sparklers.'

'I not know nutting. I fit Tools Gunstone up mit nutting an' I know nutting about no demises of no one.'

'Of course not,' I said. 'That's what I told Willy – but you know what he's like. When it comes to villainy he wouldn't trust his dear little grey-haired mother.'

'I know nutting,' Diamonds repeated gloomily.

'Like I was saying,' I said. 'I'm out a watch and I reckoned you wouldn't mind letting me have one down to the old pals act.'

He reached deep into a secret pocket in his Crombie overcoat – like a conjurer.

'You tell Villy I'm straight, OK?' he said, waving a fistful of watches under my nose.

I selected a gold Omega with a crocodile skin strap.

109

CHAPTER TWENTY ONE

A grey Gothic sky hung heavily over the country church-yard for Patrick Tomlinson's funeral and it was raining cats and dogs. Beneath a canopy of umbrellas a clutch of soberly-attired mourners clustered around the grave. The parish priest, his head bent over a prayer book, delivered the burial rite in a rapid and barely audible voice. The rain pelted down across the wind. In an effort to discourage the deluge from using his dog-collar as a drain-pipe, the priest hunched his shoulders. It was a losing battle. He was soaked to the skin and water gushed out of his trouser legs.

Lady Sonia stood alone. She had the corpse of a raven on her head and a dense black veil fell, like a curtain, over her face. Low moans filtered intermittently through the veil; now and then a delicate lace handkerchief, clutched in velvet-gloved fingers, disappeared beneath the veil and dabbed at her tear-swollen eyes.

Competing with the rain on the other side of the grave were two women I had not seen before. Snivelling happily at my elbow was Elinor. Between Tomlinson and me there was no love lost, and I was secretly relieved that someone had deprived me of the responsibility of taking my revenge on him, but I was crying too.

I'd rather face something easy, like a firing squad, than a bevy of weeping females. The tears of women have the same effect on me as old movies like *Brief Encounter*.

Elinor reached out a comforting hand and lightly squeezed my arm.

'There, there,' she sobbed. 'It's frightfully sweet of you to shed a tear, but it really isn't necessary.'

I wiped my nose on my sleeve.

The undertaker's men lowered the coffin into the grave and the priest splattered it with a handful of mud as he recited the bit about ashes to ashes. Lady Sonia tossed in a bunch of limp red roses.

The moment the incantations had come to an end, the mourners made tracks for the churchyard gate. Two ebony limousines stood waiting to take them to Bramley Hall where sherry and sandwiches had been promised. The priest squelched his sodden way to the vestry.

Clews and du Ponte had put in a predictable appearance. They were loitering by the gate, scrutinizing the mourners as they passed by.

'G'morning, Super,' I piped as I came abreast of him. 'Lovely weather for ducks.'

'Got a minute, Ed?' he asked.

'Lady Sonia has invited me for a drink.'

Clews barred my way; his tone was insistent.

'I'll give you a lift.'

It was the first time that I'd joined a funeral cortège in a police car. The way things were going it was unlikely to be the last.

For a time we sat in silence, listening to the rain pounding the roof and the rhythmical pump of the windscreen-wipers as they swung to and fro like upside-down pendulums.

Clews started the ball rolling when he was good and ready.

'Thing is, Ed,' he said, 'I am wondering which side you are on in this case.'

'Law and order, every time, Super,' I replied, quick as a flash.

He gave me a deceptively friendly smile.

'Glad to hear it. But you have to admit that you've been keeping some fairly shady company of late?'

'Like who?'

'Well, you spent a couple of hours down the Hide Away club Tuesday night. And who pays you a visit Wednesday morning but our old friend, Diamonds Silverman.'

'Contacts,' I explained. 'Just making contacts, that's all.'

'I see,' he sighed. 'Are you thinking of starting your own firm of bank robbery and jewel thieves?'

Algernon thought that was frightfully funny.

'Come off it, Super,' I said. 'You know as well as I do that if an investigator is going to get results he has to have a few reliable contacts in the underworld. Where would Scotland Yard be without grasses in the right places?'

'Look Ed, let's stop ducking and diving around the houses. You've stumbled on two corpses so far, right?'

I nodded lugubriously.

'On both occasions some very valuable jewellery has gone missing.'

'Same jewellery both times,' I put in.

'Don't interrupt the Superintendent when he's speaking,' snarled du Ponte.

'Sorry.'

Clews cleared his throat and continued.

'I'm not going to tell you everything we know, but I will tell you this. We are aware that both Willy Paradis and Diamonds Silverman had a hand in it. And we've a shrewd suspicion that they're using you as a front man.'

'Me? A front man? You must be bonkers!'

'Don't try playing the innocent with me, there's a good chap. . . .'

'What the hell you on about?'

Clews was smiling again.

'Tell you what I'll do with you.'

'What?'

'You turn Queen's evidence and I'll write around your little lapse when I make out my report . . . if not, we'll nick you as an accessory to murder.'

'Before or after the fact?' I sneered.

'Either,' said du Ponte. 'I shouldn't think we will have a great deal of difficulty in making one of them stick, what?'

I began to shiver and it wasn't just the rain soaking through to my skin.

Clews said: 'It's up to you, my lad. Talk or I'll lock you up and throw the key in the Thames.'

'But I don't know anything.'

The policemen looked at each other and then at me.

'Oh, yes, you do,' said du Ponte. 'What about the jewels?'

'What about them?'

'Has Diamonds Silverman got them?'

'Of course he bloody hasn't. You must be completely off your rocker if you think I'm involved with the murders. I don't *do* murder cases.'

'That has been puzzling us a bit, I have to admit,' said Clews. 'Divorce snooping and scouring the West End for runaway teenage girls is your speciality, isn't it?'

'That's right,' I replied eagerly. 'I'm an all-round degenerate – but I never have anything to do with murders.'

'Quite,' said du Ponte. 'You started off by trying to gather together a little evidence that might be of interest in a divorce suit and now find yourself slightly out of your depth, what?'

'Couldn't've put it better myself.'

The car drew up outside Bramley Hall. I was beginning to hate the dump.

'Just bear in mind,' said Clews as I opened the door. 'We'll only dig you out of this nasty little mess if you give us a break.'

I got out of the car.

'If you uncover anything of interest, I want to be the first to hear about it!' he called after me.

The mourners had foregathered in the library. They were sipping sherry and nibbling wafer-thin cucumber sandwiches. Mrs Dixon, the housekeeper, lurked by the door with a tray of drinks in her hand. I'd've willingly given my shoes for a shot of Hankey Bannister's, but sherry which like cheap champagne bypasses drunkenness and induces instant hangover, is the ideal beverage for solemn occasions. I grabbed a glass off the tray, sipped gingerly and surveyed the room.

The function was poorly attended. A dozen or so of Patrick's friends or relations had turned up to judge by the cut of their dark suits and the fancy black hats of the ladies who accompanied them. Lady Sonia had invited in some of the villagers who had dutifully paraded at the grave-side. They were huddled together in a corner trying to look inconspicuous and not altogether succeeding.

Elinor was draped over the mantelpiece, black crepe billowing in every direction, pouring her heart out to a tall dark stranger. She caught my eye and beckoned me over with a backward nod of her head.

'James, I want you to meet Mr Wellington.'

'Nelson,' I corrected her.

'How awful of me, I knew you were one of them,' she clucked. 'He's the private dick I was telling you about, dear . . . This is my son James.'

We shook hands, his palm was clammy. His almost latin good looks were marred by watery green eyes with blue pouches

113

under them, a receding hair line and teeth that were too small. Too much oil imposed three rigid waves on his jet black hair, brushed straight back from the temples. Under the lamps in the crystal chandelier it shone like patent leather.

'You knew Mr Tomlinson?' he said, dipping his head obsequiously.

'Not so's you'd notice,' I replied. 'Lady Sonia commanded my presence, and here I am.'

'Why?'

'Why, what?'

'Why did she command your presence?'

'Search me,' I said soothingly. He seemed to be jumpy as an alley cat.

'I fail to see why a private investigator should be invited to attend the funeral of someone to whom he is not even related.'

'Quite agree.'

'You're being frightfully rude, James,' chipped in Elinor. 'I can't think what's come over you.'

'If you must know, mother, I thoroughly dislike this distasteful function taking place in our house. Patrick Tomlinson wasn't even a member of the family. You persuaded me to come but I should like to get back to London without delay.'

'Superintendent Clews is outside in his car,' I said. 'Why don't you ask him for a lift? I'm sure he'd be overjoyed to meet you.'

He jumped about seven yards into the air – well perhaps a little less. I couldn't actually see any hair oil on the ceiling.

'They gave me a lift from the church,' I said. 'It wouldn't surprise me if they were still hanging about somewhere around the manor.'

He growled something and made a bee-line for the door. Elinor followed close behind, her crepe flapping like black wings.

I kicked a log in the grate and a shower of sparks went up the chimney. The uneasy clutch of locals were directly behind me. I lit a cigarette and plugged into their conversation.

'. . . all spit and polish, dressed as an army sergeant,' said a woman's voice.

'See,' said another. 'Couldn't've bin the gaffer, 'e was an officer.'

'I tell you it was,' a third voice insisted. 'Seen 'im plain as day.

Less than twenty yards off. I'd know 'im anywhere – we was boys together.'

' 'E nearly run my Doris over in that big green car,' put in a new more aggressive voice. 'Drivin' like a madman, 'e were, down the lane from Penny's farm. If'n Doris 'adn't jumped into the 'edge, she'd be a goner now, I'm tellin' you.'

' 'E be upset wot with the troubles,' soothed a friend. ' 'E wouldn't be 'idin' 'isself away in somun else's clothes, if 'e bain't be upset about sumut serious.'

'Rum do,' said a woman's voice.

'Now don't you go talkin', Lilly,' said a man.

I threw back what remained of my sherry in one revolting gulp. So the army sergeant, who'd done his best to wipe me off the face of the earth the other day, was none other than Sir Samford Peveril. He must definitely be a candidate for the bug hutch.

CHAPTER TWENTY-TWO

'Come with me,' said Lady Sonia, as the tail of the last car disappeared down the drive.

'Where to?'

'My room.' Without further discussion she led the way across the marble hall and along an oak-panelled passage towards the rear of the house. Halfway along she paused in front of a door and glanced around to make sure I was on her tail, then she turned the glass doorknob and entered the room. She held the door open for me, then closed it and turned the key in the lock.

'Is that to keep me in or intruders out?' Not yet having worked out who the murderer was exactly, I didn't much fancy being locked in with one of the suspects. She might've had a derringer in her garter for all I knew.

'My life is in danger,' she whispered, then hurried over to the drinks cabinet and got busy with the bottles and glasses.

Sonia's boudoir was all pink roses and tassels. Old rose lamp-shades were supported by golden dolphins and there were more than enough little feminine ornaments littered about. She must've had a right old blitz on Bond Street with an interior decorator sometime fairly recently, judging by the newness of everything. She was keeping up with the Jones's. Her ego was stamped over everything.

Sonia wasn't looking too good. The past few days had played havoc with her looks. In those good old days when I wasn't doing anything more dangerous than snooping on her love tangle, she hadn't seemed a day over thirty. Now she looked forty-five and wasn't getting any younger. Her neat honey blonde hair was a mass of rats' tails and mouse at the roots. Her make up had misfired and the fetching lace blouse she wore with her black coat and skirt was wilting.

'Drink?' she asked, half turning towards me.

'Hankey Bannister's if you have it — otherwise anything, so long as it's Scotch whisky.'

She poured two half tumblers of an anonymous brand from a crystal decanter, then discovered that the soda syphon was empty.

'We'll have to drink it neat,' she said and handed me one of the tumblers. Chucking the hard stuff on top of the funeral sherry was asking for trouble, but if Sonia was game, so was I.

'Firsht today,' she quipped and two thirds of her drink swirled down her throat like water down a drain. I realized that Lady Sonia was a lush — it was the kind of detail that a sharp-eyed private detective should've noticed sooner.

She slumped into a pink satin chair and gazed at me, bleary-eyed.

'I need protection, Mr Nelson.'

'Don't we all?' I said. 'But who from?'

'From a homoshidal maniac!' she screamed.

I winced and hoped to God that she wasn't going to fall apart. I do my best, but I'm no good at pulling people together who fall apart. I just fall apart myself.

'Do you happen to know who this homicidal maniac is?'

She swigged her whisky greedily and spoke in a torrent. The words tumbled over each other like two Irish drunks falling downstairs.

'I saw it . . . I actually saw him do it. I was standing there

116

when he killed Patrick. I screamed and ran . . . I ran and ran. He was going to kill me too. I saw it in his eyes. There's no mistaking a thing like that when you see it in a person's eyes . . . I just stumbled and ran blindly away. He was crashing through the undergrowth behind me . . . but, somehow I got to the car. I just threw myself behind the wheel . . . I couldn't see a thing, but I just drove off as fast as I could . . . I drove away down the lane. I drove for miles and miles . . . I just kept driving and praying that the awful thing I'd seen would go away . . . trying to believe it hadn't really happened . . . I must've been halfway to London before I eventually turned back.'

'So that's how you came to have sand on your shoes,' I murmured. I was very proud of myself for having picked up that clue. I even managed to forgive myself for only just realizing that she was a drinker.

'Sand?' she cried. 'I don't know anything about sand. Patrick was threatening him with a gun. He took no notice and just went for him . . . Patrick pulled the trigger several times but it never went off . . . It would've saved his life if it had.'

'Never a good idea to pinch a shooter. You don't know where it's been.'

She wasn't listening. The hair-raising yarn she was spinning me was obviously playing on her mind, and I didn't blame her.

'I know he's going to kill me – he's coming for me next,' she gasped, and made a dash for the whisky.

This time I was too quick for her. I snatched up the decanter and held it behind my back. Her panic-stricken eyes looked daggers at me.

'Give it to me!'

'Not till you tell me the name.'

She fell away from me and glowered. Then a cunning glint came into her eye.

'Come on, Ed, give 'ickle Shonia a itshy-bitshy drink.'

I prised her glass out of her fist, poured a slug of whisky and held it tantalizingly just out of her reach.

'Tell 'ickle Ed who killed Cock Robin . . . then you get 'ickle drinky.'

She tried to snatch the glass out of my hand but couldn't make it. She stared at me wild-eyed and then at the delicious

117

amber liquid. If she'd had a gun in her hand she'd've blown my brains out. Her lips began to move.

'Samford,' she breathed. 'My husband.' She held her hand out for her prize and I gave it to her.

It's always a bit tricky to tell whether a drunken woman, whose butler and lover have recently been bumped off, is levelling with you. Sonia's story was that she'd been an eye-witness to Patrick's murder and that it was her husband who'd done it. Furthermore, he was now hanging about around the neighbourhood disguised as an army sergeant and she was convinced that she was the next on his list. I knew only too well that there was some demented nut-case hanging around who answered to that description, but I was not at all sure that it was the illusive baronet. It is certainly true that double murderers tend not to be very rational, but my bet was that he'd scarpered and was now safely tucked away in his Monte Carlo hide-out waiting for Pru and Willy to clean up his act. Maybe it was a bit obvious but it was the only thing that made any sense.

When Sonia'd tossed off her drink and replenished her glass, she outlined her plans for me.

'Body-guard . . . that'sh wha' I need.'

'Me too.'

She either didn't hear or chose to ignore that remark and started to grope about in the drawer of a flashy repro escritoire. She came up with a wad of notes and tossed them into my lap. They were twenties and there seemed to be a lot of them.

She slumped back into her chair, all forlorn.

'You musht protect me,' she implored. 'If you refuse I will be murdered and 'ish'll be your fault.'

'That,' I told her, 'is moral blackmail.'

'Don't care wha'sh call it.'

'Now, now,' I pleaded, 'for goodness sake don't start blubbing. You must give me time to think this out.'

I fingered the notes thoughtfully, trying to reach a snap decision. Willy and Pru had told me to get close to Sonia and find out what was buzzing. Clews had put the frighteners on me with the accessory threat. Someone, I still wasn't sure who, was going around rubbing people out and I didn't much fancy getting in the light. With Tomlinson no longer around, Willy, who had a good deal of experience in disposing of people he didn't like, was now the front runner on my short list of suspects. On balance, keeping in with him seemed the best way of saving my own skin.

I pocketed the notes and told Sonia that I'd stick around, but that she shouldn't expect too much from me if we ended up in any tight corners. A little later we left her boudoir and went back to the library.

Mrs Dixon was clearing away the sherry glasses and Elinor was studying a gardening encyclopedia. She looked up as we came in and said: 'Ah, there you are – I was beginning to wonder what had become of you two.'

Lady Sonia knocked over a lampstand and said: 'I've jusht been showing mishter Nelshon over the housh.'

Mrs Dixon headed swiftly across the room with a tray of glasses. She paused at the door and addressed the room.

'None of us will be safe in our beds until the police have got the murderer behind bars,' she declared. 'How many for dinner?'

Sonia gave me a quick glance and then turned to Elinor.

'I shall be returning to town with mishter Nelshon,' she said. 'Would you like to come with ush?'

'I must get the Hybrid Trollius bedded out this afternoon,' replied Elinor good-naturedly. 'I couldn't possibly come to London.'

Mrs Dixon leaned against the door jamb. Sonia smiled at her and said: 'Jusht one for dinner, mishes Dixon.'

'Sloshed again,' sniffed the housekeeper and stalked off.

I mentioned in passing that I ought to pay Mr Goodway, the village garage proprietor, a visit to see if he'd carried out the plastic surgery on my car. I asked Lady Sonia if I could give him a ring.

'You are not to leave my shide,' she screamed. 'You mushn't leave me alone, even for a minute – my life ish in danger you undershtand? MY–LIFE–ISH–IN–DANGER!'

Elinor looked on with a faintly amused expression on her face.

'Why not telephone the garage and ask them to deliver it?' she suggested.

'What a splendid idea,' I ventured at last.

119

CHAPTER TWENTY-THREE

The chances of Lady Sonia getting herself done in at the hairdresser's seemed pretty remote, but it was only by pulling a fast one that I succeeded in escaping from her clutches for an hour or two. One of the least attractive conditions of my employment was that I move into the Peverils' Belgravia town house, and another was her insistence that I follow her around all over the place like a devoted Labrador. Hanging around someone who thinks they are going to get murdered at any minute has few rewards. Even the three hundred smackers she'd laid on me, and the promise of three hundred more if the law captured the killer before he got to her, made the assignment only fractionally more acceptable.

She'd begun by demanding that I sit in the waiting-room until she'd had her hair done. I told her it might tarnish her image if I did that – the other ladies would run away with the idea that I was her gigolo. She agreed to let me keep an eye on the place from the café across the street. The moment she turned her back I did a bunk. There are times when a private detective has to take chances.

I looked through my post and discovered that I hadn't won the football pools. Then dialled Pru's number.

'Have a nice time at the funeral?'

'It was pretty deadly,' I replied sourly.

She said: 'Come on! It can't've been as bad as all that.'

I said: 'Yes, it was.'

She said: 'Tell me about it.'

'For a start it was raining cats and dogs. Second, Clews and du Ponte sidled up to me and mentioned in passing that they were thinking of arresting me for murder. Third, Sonia offered me a job.'

'You sound resentful,' she said. 'What was that you said about Clews?'

'Oh nothing much,' I replied airily. 'It's simply that it seems to have crossed his mind that your father and Diamonds have taken to bumping people off all over the place.' I let it sink in, but I don't think she batted an eyelid. 'The Superintendent has decided to run me in for being a friend of theirs.'

120

She didn't reply right away, but when she did she exploded:
'What ridiculous bloody nonsense!'

'Tell that to Clews. He won't listen to me.' She took no notice.
'It makes me sick,' she grumbled. 'They take it for granted that just because Daddy was a bit of a lad, in his youth, he is still up to all kinds of villainy. He runs a high-class gambling den and they've never been able to pin anything on him, or Diamonds for that matter. That's always got up Clews' nose, so I suppose they are now going to try and frame them.'

'There wouldn't be anything very unusual about that,' I commented mildly. 'By the way, it's on the cards that they've tumbled who you are.'

'I doubt it,' she snapped. 'I've refused to talk to them, you know.' I didn't know, but it sounded sensible.

She changed the subject and asked what it was that I was doing for Sonia.

'Spot of body-guard work,' I said.

'That's marvellous. Now you'll really be able to keep tabs on her.'

'You could say so,' I replied severely. 'But I want you to know that I'm doing it for the sake of you and your dad. I don't expect you'll be surprised to learn that I happen to be fractionally more blind terrified of your father than I am of the unknown murderer or even Clews. I'm counting on you two to keep me in the land of the living.'

'Don't be so silly, Ed,' she giggled. 'Daddy wouldn't hurt a fly.'

'I've known lots of flies who wouldn't agree with you.'

She laughed heartily.

'Look, I must dash, will you phone me tonight?'

'As soon as her Ladyship's passed out.'

'What on earth do you mean?'

'She's got a monumental drink problem.'

'Oh that!' said Pru, and hung up. I reached for the Hankey Bannister's and poured myself three fingers.

'To the ladies,' I toasted silently, and took a hefty gulp.

Suddenly, there was an almighty crash upstairs that seemed to shake the entire building. It was followed by angry voices. Hotpants was open for business and it sounded as though business was brisk.

121

I crept stealthily to my door, opened it a crack and sneaked a peak outside. A moment or two later a pair of ponces I knew by sight came bowling down the stairs with a battered city type struggling in their arms.

'It ain't nice when a geezer goes poachin' on uvva people's lively'ood, Mr Tomlinson,' one ponce barked wolfishly down the battered geezer's ear hole. 'Just because yuh buy a scrubber a soddin' bed don't give yuh no entitlement to no free access. Tryin' to get a bit of nookie wivout payment is like takin' the bread outta our mouves!'

His companion underlined the denouncement roundly by fetching off their victim another right hander.

It dawned on me that I'd misjudged my new neighbour. The possibility of there being more than one Patrick Tomlinson in this world hadn't even crossed my mind. There were probably dozens of them in the telephone directory.

When the nasty little contingent had disappeared from sight, I dodged upstairs and knocked on her door.

A voice shrilled over the blare of a stereo.

'It's open.'

I opened the door and went in.

At waist level on the wall opposite was a long mirror. Reflected in the mirror was the Slumberland divan. The divan was covered with a flouncy candlewick bedspread and a quantity of soft cuddly toys. Sitting cross-legged in their midst was Black Satin Hotpants eating a banana.

She gave me a fetching smile, said: 'Hi, Ed,' and bit an inch off the end of the banana.

She was wearing a wispy baby-doll nightie you could read through and nothing under it.

She pouted her sexy little stomach at me and grinned hugely.

'Cummon, Ed, lock the flippin' door,' she said. 'And let's get at it – it's on the house.'

Ten minutes later I made my weak-kneed way down stairs. There was the sound of footsteps coming up. Her next client? I paused at my door mildly curious. The well-tailored figure of a bowler-hatted gent hove into view. My face turned green and a light sweat broke out on my brow. It was Elinor's son, James.

CHAPTER TWENTY-FOUR

Lady Sonia was livid. She'd had to get all the way home from the hairdresser on her tod, expecting to get sapped, knifed, run over or plugged by a stray bullet at every turn.

Fear of getting bumped off, coupled with the enmity she was feeling towards me, kept her off the juice, and the evening proved pretty sticky.

Sitting down to eat, with only one other person, at a dining-table the size of a bowling alley is an unnerving experience at the best of times. With Sonia stone-cold sober and doing her nut, I didn't think I could take it. So, in the hope that she'd fall off the wagon with a resounding crash, I resolved to set her an example.

Having armed myself with a brimming tumbler of neat whisky, I quaffed it with the *hors d'oeuvres*, chased it with the best part of a bottle of *Liebfraumilch* over the trout and spurned the dessert in favour of brandy.

My strategy had no effect. Pale, remote, frightened and angry, she sipped a glass of wine and showed no inclination to join me in the booze-up. After supper she retired to the drawing room and sat watching the TV. I helped myself to frequent slugs of brandy and kept her company. She wasn't even speaking to me by now. When she didn't switch off after the ten o'clock news, I'd had enough. I grunted my disapproval, stuck the brandy bottle under my arm and, kicking over an occasional table that happened to get in my light, I tottered off to bed.

In the dead of night, when all was quiet and the coast was clear, I crept out of Parkhurst's room, fully dressed, and stole silently down the stairs. Lady Sonia had allotted me the dead butler's quarters – to that extent she'd classified me as hired help. Her assurances that I'd be 'perfectly comfortable' were wide of the mark. The room was cold and uncomforting, and kipping in a dead man's bed gave me the creeps.

Down in the drawing-room I fumbled the phone off the hook by the light of a match, and dialled Pru's number. The bell at the other end of the line rang once only before her voice came in my ear saying: 'Ed, is that you?'

Startled by the speed with which she'd snatched up the

receiver I said: 'Who else rings up girls in the middle of the night?'

'Something awful has happened,' she squawked. 'Something absolutely dreadful.'

'The chancellor of the exchequer has increased the tax on booze and fags again?'

'Diamonds has been murdered.'

The darkness closed in on me and an icy hand gripped my heart. If I'd been able to feel anything, I'd've been shocked and cast down by the news of Diamonds' sudden demise. But frozen fear, the private detective's most chilling adversary, had paralysed my senses. I felt nothing.

A hoarse, scared voice that I didn't recognize said: 'When did it happen, where, why, whodunnit?'

'The police found him face down in an alley with a pearl-handled dagger buried to the hilt between his shoulder blades.' Prudence Pride was not Willy Paradis' daughter for nothing. 'Gloria is helping the police with their enquiries.'

She seemed to know a hell of a lot more about it than a good girl should.

'How come you know so many of the gory details?' I asked.

For an instant she hesitated.

'Daddy phoned me half an hour ago.'

I recalled Willy's merry quip in the Hide Away about filling in the help, and a little shiver crawled up my spine. I wasn't sure that I liked being on their side.

'Are you okay?' I enquired lamely. 'Do you want me to come over?'

'I'll be all right.' There was the merest trace of a laugh. 'Daddy's put a couple of his muscle boys on my door, and two more down in the street to keep an eye on who comes in and out of the mews. Ring me in the morning. Perhaps we can have lunch.'

CHAPTER TWENTY-FIVE

My body was slick with nervous perspiration. My shirt and trousers and even my shoes were saturated with it. I squelched over to the drinks table, gulped a couple of mouthfuls of whisky straight from the decanter and then squelched upstairs.

I stripped naked, climbed into Parkhurst's narrow bed and went spark out the moment my head touched the pillow.

I had a terrible dream. Sir Samford Peveril and Parkhurst were in mortal combat on the edge of a cliff. Blood was dripping from open wounds on their bodies and their faces were beaten to a pulp. Suddenly, out of a swirling mist, a 1926 armour-plated limousine drove up. It was a Duesenberg double-cowl phaeton; behind the wheel was Pru, got up like a 'twenties vamp. She was laughing hysterically. Seated next to her, wearing a straw boater, was Willy Paradis. He too was laughing hysterically. The car screeched to a halt, the doors snapped open and a bunch of bad-faced killers piled out. One cradled a tommygun, another was armed with a sawn-off shot-gun, another a rifle, another a pistol. From their midst emerged Patrick Tomlinson in white tie, tails and an opera hat. Sir Samford and Parkhurst stared at him with hideous eyes. Tomlinson produced a jewelled derringer from his crotch and plugged a neat hole between their eyes. They toppled over the edge of the cliff and plummeted into the rocky gorge below.

I awoke screaming. Standing over me with a cup of tea in her hand was Mrs Brown.

'Bad dream?' she enquired.

'No worse than usual,' I groaned.

She placed the cup on the bedside table and looked me over.

'You must have a very guilty conscience,' she said. 'Only people with guilty consciences have bad dreams.'

'Nobody's on the legit,' I came back at her, quoting Al Capone.

She smoothed out the wrinkles in the flowered pinafore which covered her ample haunches and departed with a puzzled expression on her face.

I sipped the tea appreciatively. It was hot, strong and sweet — just the way I like it. Having early-morning tea brought to my room was the only condition I'd stuck out for when I agreed to stay in the house.

Breakfast with Lady Sonia had more to be said for it than dining with her. It took place in the breakfast-room, a bright airy room at the front of the house, facing the morning sun.

We sipped coffee and munched toast at a table that people had almost certainly sipped coffee and munched toast at during the reign of George III. The chairs we sat on must, at one time, have encased refined bustles and elegant frock coats – and Lloyd George, most likely, knew the father of the potter who made the marmalade dish.

On the wall facing the bow windows hung a rural landscape in a heavy gilt frame. Neither the picture nor its frame were made yesterday. The window looked out onto the flower garden in the middle of the square. Leaning up against a lamp-post on the corner of the street was a heavily built man, wearing a big black overcoat and a wide brimmed stetson hat over his eyes.

Sonia had on a pretty flowered dress and she seemed to have got out of the right side of the bed for a change.

'What are your plans for the day?' I asked as she poured me a second cup of coffee.

'I absolutely must do some shopping at Harrods this morning,' she said. 'Then I have to be at the Inner Temple by one. I'm lunching with Rupert.'

'Who's he?'

'Sir Rupert Worthington-Smythe, our family solicitor.'

I guessed that she wanted to make sure that her husband hadn't crossed her out of his will before his disappearance. 'Well, you won't need me around for that,' I said, quick as a flash.

'I suppose not,' she said. 'But I shall expect you to collect me from Rupert's chambers at two-thirty.'

I gave her a winning smile and said: 'You couldn't make it three o'clock, could you?'

'Very well,' she replied grudgingly, 'but no later.'

I nodded my agreement, lit a cigarette and glanced out of the window. The heavily-built man in the big black overcoat was still holding up the lamp-post on the corner.

While Sonia ducked and dived her way around Harrods' department store, I got Pru on the blower. I outlined my schedule and invited her to lunch.

'Tell you what,' she said, 'why don't you drop that bitch off at her lawyer's office, or wherever it is you're dropping her off – you can drop her in the Thames, for all I care – then come around to my place and I'll knock you up an omelet?'

It was heartening to find her, too, on such good form.

'Okay,' I said, 'But I'd be grateful if you'd mention to those barrel-bodied gorillas you've got staked out around the place, that you're expecting company. Some of your daddy's friends have been known to rough people up who mean them no harm.'

She laughed and said: 'You are an ass, Ed,' and hung up.

My face and the upper half of my body completely obscured by parcels, I barged my way out of the department store and staggered blindly along the street. Lady Sonia trotted along at my side with a hand resting lightly on my arm as though guiding a blind man.

'Which way's the car?'

'Just around the corner on the right,' she said. 'It isn't very far.'

I said: 'They're slipping – I'll drop the lot in a minute.'

'No, you won't,' she replied sternly. 'Come along.'

It wasn't until we got to the 1100 that it happened. Her ladyship's packages got away from me, and tumbled into the gutter, as I searched first in one pocket and then another for the keys. A jar of Beluga caviare smashed to smithereens at my feet and a tin of Bath Oliver biscuits rolled out into the middle of the road and got run over by a taxi.

'You clumsy clot. Now look what you've done.'

'You employed me as a bodyguard. Not a pack mule.'

She gave me the kind of scornful look that females have been giving me all my life and said: 'Is it too much for a lady to ask a gentleman to carry her parcels?'

CHAPTER TWENTY-SIX

Loitering on the corner of Pru's mews, as inconspicuously as pork chops in a synagogue, was a brace of disagreeable-looking gents with a pronounced lack of forehead, scowling, rubbery faces, short legs and dangling arms. Their mouths were plugged with Havana cigars and their thick, bulging bodies were swathed in rather too much overcoat. They presented a sinister image, which was not altogether unfamiliar.

I drew up beside them and wound down the window. I put on my most winning smile and said: 'Am I on the right road for the Victoria and Albert Museum?'

A dumb expression passed over their sallow faces. The hand of one slid under his overcoat and moved across his chest to his armpit holster. The other moved in for a closer look at me.

'Just a joke,' I said. 'I know this is not the right road for the Victoria and Albert – just a joke, funny ha ha, right?'

'Wot the bleedin' 'ell d'yuh want?'

'Ed Nelson,' I told him, 'my name is Ed Nelson – I've an appointment with Miss Pride.'

His partner stepped forward and put in his two-pennyworth.

'Nelson, does 'e reckon 'is name is?'

The other nodded. I sank down behind the steering wheel and tried to look small.

' 'E's okay, I s'pose,' continued the one with the armpit holster. He jerked a thumb over his shoulder. 'She's expectin' 'im.'

The other laughed – a nasty laugh that came from the deep black pit of his gut and erupted out of his mouth like a roar of thunder.

' 'E don't look so tough, do 'e?' he guffawed. 'I fought private dicks was s'posed t' be so tough?'

I tapped my forehead with an index finger.

'I'm tough in the mind,' I said. 'Like Albert Einstein and Sigmund Freud.'

He bit his lip and scratched his head thoughtfully.

'Who a dey, tearaways on the Kray firm?'

'You've just won a colour TV set and a holiday for two in the Balearics,' I told him, and drove into the mews.

Two more gorillas, in two more emblematic overcoats, stood

sentinel at Pru's front door. They eyed me suspiciously as I alighted from the car. I approached smiling and gave them the password: 'Ed Nelson.'

One grunted and the other pounded on the door with a balled fist. Neither took their eyes off me.

The door opened and Pru appeared on the doorstep. She had on a white silk blouse, black calf length skirt and wedge espadrilles. Her hair hung loosely about her shoulders and she was smiling prettily.

'You actually made it! How lovely. Come in and have a drink.'

Her father's hounds fell apart, like the Red Sea, and I strolled between them into the house.

She led the way into her little sitting-room. I'd been in it before, but it looked different somehow. It was daylight, I suppose.

'Whisky?' she asked.

'Hankey Bannister's?'

'I bought a bottle especially for you,' she said. 'You'd be amazed how difficult it is to get.'

It was a relief to find myself still in favour.

'Any news of the Silverman killing?' I asked. 'Have the law nabbed the culprit yet?'

She gave me a funny look, handed me my drink and replied carelessly.

'I expect Daddy'll know. He should be here in a minute. He's joining us for lunch.'

No romantic little lunch *à deux*, I concluded, and resolved to drink little and watch my p's and q's.

Half an hour drifted broodily by before our cosy chat was rudely interrupted by several hefty thumps on the front door.

Up sprang Pru, almost out of her skin.

She returned shortly in the shadow of her father. He was suavely turned out in an olive green suit, cream shirt, maroon silk tie, a pearl-grey felt hat and brown-and-white *co-respondents'* shoes. He seemed neither delighted nor irritated to find me there. He looked at me the way gangsters do and said:

'Wotcha, Ed, 'ow's tricks?'

I smiled affably and shrugged.

129

'So who's going to listen if I complain?'

Willy liked that and laughed.

'You're a born loser, Ed.' His tone held no offence. 'A born loser.'

I waved the bottle of Hankey Bannister's at him and asked if he wanted some.

He shook his head.

'Never drink when I'm on the job. You shouldn't eeva.'

'I know,' I said and replenished my glass. Then added: 'Sorry to hear about poor old Diamonds cashing in his chips.'

'Yeah,' sighed Willy, 'that's a bit a monkey business that's gonna need some cunnin' fort.'

He settled himself in a chair and looked me over appraisingly.

'This one's got the feminine touch to it. Shive merchants don't go around tooled up wiv pearl 'andled daggers. Where was 'er ladyship last night?'

'At home,' I answered confidently. Then I was assailed by doubt. 'Until ten-thirty, anyway. She'd got the dead needle and was watching the box. I went to bed before all the late night sex 'n' violence came on.'

'Was she drinking?' asked Pru.

'She kept off it last night, surprisingly enough.'

Willy and Pru exchanged meaningful glances. I was beginning to feel choked off with the pair of them.

'I'm sick of this case,' I said and set light to another fag. 'Everyone is accusing everyone else. I'm beginning to think you all had a hand in it like *Murder on the Orient Express*.'

Willy glanced at Pru.

'Wot's 'e on about?'

'A whodunnit by Agatha Christie,' said Pru.

'Never 'eard of 'er.'

'I wouldn't expect you to have.' The whisky was getting to me despite my good resolution.

Pru said: 'Don't be rude to my father.'

Willy grinned all over his ugly mug.

'It's OK, sugar. Ed didn't mean no offence.'

'That's right,' I mumbled. 'I didn't mean any offence.'

Willy smiled, his rubber-lipped, menacing smile – I fought off the impulse to jump up and run blindly out of the house.

'Now you listen to me, loser,' he said, 'an' listen good.'

I listened good.

'This little business 'as bin 'angin' about so long it's beginnin' to look untidy. The linens are 'avin' a field day and Clews is startin' to poke around too close to 'ome. So the full strength is I've decided to steam in and the fun and games ain't gonna go on no longer. We're gonna get this fing tidied up and outta the light on the 'urry up and no more larkin' about. If yuh wonna job done, do itcha self, right?'

I looked into his eyes – ice-blue. Ice cold. He meant it and it was no skin off my nose.

I nodded mutely.

'No one else ain't gonna get done in,' he continued, 'and I'm gonna 'and someone over to Clews on a plate.'

'Anyone I know?' I enquired acidly.

'Maybe,' said Willy. 'Maybe not. Let me put it this way – when I switch on the telly and see people bumpin' each uvver off all over the place, I reckon they're liable to 'ave a good reason and it ain't none of my business anyway.' He lowered his voice and stroked Pru's arm affectionately. 'But when it comes to blades and shooters on my manor, and me own are in the line of fire, stands to reason I gotta close ranks a bit – just like them politicians do when it comes out that the Prime Minister is screwin' 'is secretary. Am I right or wrong?'

Pru let out a shrill little laugh.

It was only fear of looking a burk that prevented me from doing the same.

'No doubt about it, Willy,' I said. 'You've definitely got a point.'

CHAPTER TWENTY-SEVEN

It didn't happen when I least expected it to. Nothing that happens at three a.m. is unexpected. The bark of a fox, the screech of an owl, the distant wail of a police siren or the steady footfall of a brace of plod treading their lonely beat are all sounds that the trained ear can expect to pick up at three a.m. and so is the creak of stairs.

I pricked up my ears, like a terrier. I may not've been much of a credit to my profession – some people might even have gone so far as to say that I was a worthless, drunken, nicotine-stained lowlife and I'd've more than half-way agreed with them. But I'd never in my life been wrong about the ominous sound of creaking stairs. A moment or two later it came again.

I slipped out of bed, pulled on my dressing-gown and felt around in the dark for the shillelagh that I'd taken to sleeping with lately. It made the bed lumpy and was not as cuddly to go to bed with as a glamorous blonde. But in the circumstances it was a damn sight better than going to bed alone.

I tip-toed across the room, opened the door a crack and peered out at the landing. It was dark, but enough street light filtered through the window at the end of the passage for me to see that there was no one there. I waited and listened. A minute crept silently by and no more creaks came from the stairs.

With my shillelagh at the ready, I slipped out of the room and stole noiselessly to the head of the stairs. There was nothing there but yawning darkness and graveyard silence. I leaned against the banister rail and strained my ears for the slightest sound. An icy wind scythed across the nape of my neck, the massed band of the Brigade of Guards split my ear drums, my brains spiralled into a whirlpool and a silly cinema featured highlights of my mis-spent youth.

When I came to, a watery dawn light beamed through the landing window like a searchlight cone. A second head, the size of a coconut, had swelled up behind my left ear. My mind was a wasteland and I was suffering from double vision. And it wasn't the nice rosy double vision you get from alcohol.

I passed a hand over my face, rolled over, and struggled painfully on to my hands and knees. There was a dark stain on the carpet where my head had been. Blood.

I puked . . . more blood. The rotter had booted me in the kidneys.

I flip-flopped head first down the stairs on my belly like a turtle. It was twice as tough as swimming the English Channel.

132

Swimming downstairs always was tougher than swimming in water.

At the foot of the stairs I managed somehow to get to my feet, and walking sort of bent over, I wobbled across the hall and went into the drawing-room.

A drop of brandy restored the circulation, but there seemed no way of putting a stop to the firework display that was taking place behind my eyes. I slumped into an armchair and tried to think. I couldn't think about anything except how much my head hurt. I heaved myself out of the chair, stumbled over to a wall mirror and took a squint at my own worst enemy. I looked as bad as I felt.

I sipped a little more brandy; the firework display subsided long enough for me to dial Willy's number. The bell at the other end of the line rang for an eternity. Then a gravelly, yawning voice said: 'Mr Paradis' residence.'

'Can I speak to him?' My voice was a lot quieter and calmer than I had expected it to be.

'Who's speakin'?'

'The North Thames Gas Board,' I said. 'There's a leak in your street and the whole area has got to be evacuated.'

There was a stony silence, followed by a clatter as he put the receiver down on a hard surface. A minute or so later Willy came on the line.

' 'Allo!' he rasped. 'What the 'ell's this all about then?'

I said: 'It's me.'

'Who?' he said.

I said: 'Me, Ed Nelson.'

'Do yuh 'appen to know wot time it soddin' well is?'

'It's soddin' well time I blew down Clews' earhole – that's what time it is.'

'You pissed?' he enquired icily.

In the heat of the moment I completely forgot who I was speaking to.

'Listen, you slag,' I snarled. 'How come you sent one of your tearaways around here to rub me out?'

Willy let out a rasping laugh.

'You are pissed,' he said. 'Or else you've gone off yuh rocker. Why would I wanna send someone around to give yuh the business? Only yesterday afternoon I made meself yuh silent partner.'

'I know you, you dirty rat. You bung your victims a load of old moody, stick 'em in the land of promise, then hit 'em on the nut with an iron bar when their back's turned.'

Like all real gangsters Willy carried guilt, insecurity, pride and fear around on his shoulder in the shape of a chip. I'd got him on the raw, insulted his integrity. He was deeply offended.

'Listen to me, punk,' he blazed. 'I'm gonna break a 'abit of a life time an' tell yuh the full strengf, right?'

'I'm listening.'

'I don't know nothin' about wotcha on about. If some finger 'as been duffin' yuh up – I don't know who it is and I don't give a monkies. I've got the Peveril gaff staked out, as it 'appens. So if some geezer 'as been doin' a bit of breakin' and enterin' the boys'll've clocked 'im an' 'e ain't gonna get far, got it?'

'Got it,' I said.

CHAPTER TWENTY-EIGHT

The clock in the hall struck seven. I eased myself out of the chair and returned gingerly to my room. I made a swift check to see if the motive for the assault was robbery. The thin wad of notes between me and the workhouse was still in my trousers' hip pocket and Diamonds' Omega watch was still on the bedside table. The motive had not been robbery. Of course it sodding well hadn't, it'd been homicide! I hurried out of the room, stumbled along the landing and hammered on the door of the master bedroom. There was no reply. I hammered again and rattled the handle. The door was locked.

'Lady Sonia!' I shouted and kept right on hammering.

'Lady Sonia! Speak to me, speak to me!'

'What on earth is it?' came a petulant voice from inside.

'Sonia,' I gasped, 'are you all right?'

'Who is it, for heaven's sake?'

'Ed Nelson.'

134

'What do you want?'

'Are you all right?'

'What do you mean by waking me up at this hour in the morning to ask if I'm all right?'

'All part of the service, ma'm,' I said and returned to my room.

I felt fractionally better for a hot bath and a shave. I noticed as I combed my hair that the egg behind my ear was turning blue. Kidneys pickled in alcohol have tremendous recuperative powers, but they draw the line at a kicking. There was a technicolour bruise in the small of my back, where the unpleasant fellow had put the boot in and my rib cage wasn't feeling too good either, but all in all I was in better shape than I might've been if he'd really meant it. It began to look very much as though I was going to be around when the next hooligan took it into his head to rough me up.

Sonia rebuked me with her eyes as I came into the breakfast room and I thought for a moment that she was going to take me to task about the alarm call. But something changed her mind, her face blanched and she said: 'Good God, what happened to you?'

'Ran into the phantom you've been expecting,' I said. 'He was lurking about on the stairs in the wee small hours.'

I sat down at the table and glanced out of the window. Willy's strong-arm was still in evidence, slouched up against a lamp-post on the corner of the street. There was another one loitering on the right hand side of the square. I wondered why they'd been on the missing list when I needed them.

Sonia gazed at me blankly. She had her elbows on the table and was trembling all over. The crockery and assorted cutlery rattled as though an earthquake was imminent.

'Get me a drink,' she gasped. 'I can't stand it, I tell you. Get me a drink!'

She was falling apart at the seams and although I don't approve of ladies who drink before the lunch-hour session, I got up and shuffled off to the drawing-room in search of the restorative. I came back into the room, brandy bottle in hand, to find myself looking down the muzzle of a pretty little pearl-handled pistol.

135

I dropped the bottle and started to back out.

'Stay where you are!' commanded Sonia. Her teeth flashed in a smile, brief as a roll of dice.

'I rather think I shall not be ñeeding your services any longer, Mr Nelson,' she said.

I smiled too, a clammy, leering smile that a condemned man might give the hangman as they exchange a no-hard-feelings handshake on the steps of the scaffold.

'Fine,' I said, 'absolutely fine. Whatever you say is absolutely fine with me, your ladyship.'

She stroked the barrel of the gun and moved the muzzle up a bit so that it pointed right between my eyes.

'You have outlived your usefulness, Mr Nelson.' Her voice was calm, cool and collected and strangely without menace.

I mustered a tragic expression.

'Look here,' I croaked, taking care to be more than polite. 'Maybe I'm not the best private detective in the world. In fact I'm quite prepared to admit that I'm the worst – actually I'm not really qualified to be a private eye at all. Just filling in 'til something more worth while comes along.'

I reached into my hip pocket. She studied me closely but made no effort to stop me. I tossed the remains of her retainer on the floor at her feet.

'There you are, there's your money back – I'll return the rest of it to you just as soon as I can. You have my solemn oath on that . . .'

'You're despicable, Mr Nelson,' she sneered, lowering the gun. 'Kindly pour me a brandy.'

I retrieved the bottle from the floor and hurried to her side, eager to be of service. I splashed a hefty slug into her coffee cup. She lifted it to her lips and drank greedily. The effect was satisfactory.

'I've decided to let you live,' she announced. 'You're a nasty little worm but you're not worth killing. Pick up your money and get out before I change my mind.'

A decidedly fishy turn of events, I thought, as I stuffed my few belongings into a plaid zip bag. She was entitled to dispense with my services if she no longer felt the need of them. But she'd chosen a pretty outlandish way of doing it.

Something was pretty niffy in the state of Denmark.

Sonia was waiting for me at the foot of the stairs when I came down. She had a fixed smile on her face like the Queen Mother musters when she pays a state visit to a North Country iron foundry.

'Be seeing you then,' I said as I came abreast of her.

The smile remained fixed.

'I think it extremely unlikely, Mr Nelson.'

I said: 'You never know your luck, your ladyship' and offered my hand.

She touched it lightly and led the way to the front door. We'd got half way when the telephone on the hall table started to ring. I grabbed the receiver and put it to my ear.

'Peveril residence,' I said.

'That you, Ed?'

'Hello, Willy,' I said, 'kind of you to call.'

'We captured the geezer wot duffed yuh up.'

'Have you really,' I replied cheerily. 'That certainly is good news. Where are you exactly?'

Sonia stood a short distance away with an eager expression on her face. Still eyeing her I said: 'Aldershot! What on earth are you doing in Aldershot?'

Sonia's face turned the colour of bathroom tiles.

Willy said: 'We've got 'im in an upstairs room in a boozer.' He shouted to his henchmen. 'Wot's the name of this boozer?'

The muffled voice said: 'The 'Arf Moon.'

'The 'Arf Moon,' said Willy.

'The Half Moon,' I said. 'Where is it exactly?'

'Where is it?' shouted Willy.

A muffled voice rattled off what sounded like directions. Willy came back on the line: 'Paxton Street, Aldershot. Second on yuh right after the barracks. Yuh shoot down the M4 to Readin' then belt through Farnborough and yuh wind up at Aldershot. About fifty miles from the smoke. Yuh oughta make it in one, maybe two hours.'

'I know where it is all right,' I replied grimly. 'Did a bit of my National Service there, as it happens.'

'Getcha skates on,' he said and hung up.

I cradled the receiver and turned to Sonia. She knew a damn

137

sight better than I did that the jig was up. She gazed at me glassy-eyed, saying nothing.

'Well, bye-bye, Lady Sonia,' I said. 'I'd better be on my way.'

'Please wait a moment, Mr Nelson,' she whispered. 'Please wait . . .'

I waited.

She moistened her lips and moved a little closer to me.

'Mr Nelson, you absolutely must listen to me,' she pleaded.

'I'm listening.'

'I want to come with you.'

CHAPTER TWENTY-NINE

The plucky 1100 buzzed like an angry wasp along the main drag and overtook everything in sight. The cars we passed had many more horses under their bonnets than we had. But we were in rather a hurry.

Sonia sat stony-faced at my side. From time to time she took a hefty swig from a hip flask she kept in her handbag. It seemed to steady her nerves, but she didn't offer me any. I wondered idly if she also had the pearl-handled pistol in her purse.

About ten miles from the Aldershot turn-off I swerved into a filling-station and told the attendant to fill her up and check the oil. We needed a quart of oil. My car burned nearly as much oil as petrol.

Rising like a monument to bad taste, a short distance from the petrol pumps, was a ghastly neon-lit complex of buildings. Signs said: 'CAFETERIA. CIGARETTES. TELEPHONES. LADIES and GENTS.'

'Won't be a minute,' I told Sonia. 'I need a packet of smokes.'

She gave me a zombie-like look and said nothing.

I smiled apologetically, removed the keys from the ignition and got out of the car.

I bought a packet of fags at the kiosk, nipped into the gents for a quick slash and then almost as an afterthought I popped into a call box and phoned the Yard.

Clews was out sleuthing, but I managed to get in a quick word edgeways with Algernon du Ponte. He lost his temper when I invited both him and the superintendent to join me for a drink in the Half Moon at Aldershot.

'Where?' he hollered.

'The Half Moon at Aldershot.'

'If this is intended to be some kind of joke,' he intoned, 'I must say that it is in frightfully poor taste and it will be my pleasure to see that you are brought to book. You may be absolutely certain of that, you ghastly little chiseller.'

It was the kind of insult that I got often but never got used to.

'You coming or aren't you? Like they say in the personal columns: you may discover something to your advantage.'

'I'll swing for you yet,' said Algernon.

'Mind it ain't from your old school tie,' I said and rang off.

Why I hadn't expected Lady Sonia to take a powder on me I can't imagine. But when I got back to the car and found that she'd gone, I was genuinely surprised. The bash on the nut must've scrambled my grey matter worse than I thought.

To begin with I thought she might've been paying a visit to the 'Ladies', but when after five minutes she failed to put in an appearance I strolled over to the pump attendant and asked if by any chance he'd seen her.

He grinned from ear to ear.

'That lardydar bit in the mink and head scarf?'

'That's right.'

'Gorn, ain't she?'

'Where?'

'Went orf wiv a young fella in a red sports car, didn't she?'

I was in no mood for his native cockney wit. Its charm was completely lost on me. Any more of it and I'd douse him with petrol from his own nozzle and set light to him.

'Which way'd they go?' I rasped.

'Don't know, do I?'

I turned on my heel and marched back to the 1100.

The Half Moon in Paxton Street, Aldershot, turned out to be a vast grey Victorian building, with turrets at the corners of the roof. The turrets were dotted with gargoyles and griffins. I could've been wrong; they might've been Willy Paradis' team of

139

tearaways gazing down at me. But they certainly looked like gargoyles and griffins.

A well-worn, highly polished, brass plate on the door said: PUSH. I shoved it open and sauntered into a long L-shaped bar with my hands hanging loosely at my sides hoping I looked like a gun-fighter.

The nicotine-stained wallpaper was dotted with military insignias. It was obviously the Aldershot squaddies' local. If further indication was needed, there was, at the far end of the room, a stage on which was a piano. Above the piano was a notice printed in bold black capitals: NO DANCING, SINGING OR FIGHTING. Behind the bar was a second notice: DON'T ASK FOR CREDIT AS A REFUSAL OFTEN OFFENDS.

Holding up the opposite end of the bar were two men. One was a big man with heavy shoulders and a battered brooding face; the other was short and stocky, built like a fighting cock. They both wore snap-brimmed felt hats and looked as though they were angry with the world about something. I'd seen them around, but didn't know their names.

'Your name Nelson?' asked the little fighting cock.

'Who wants to know?' I kept smiling.

The big man towered over me.

'Wotcha self, mug,' he warned. 'If the kid arsts yuh yuh name, jist tell 'im nice an' polite, like.'

'Kid,' I said. 'My name's Nelson.'

The kid pointed at the ceiling.

'The guv'nor's waitin' on yuh,' he informed me out of the corner of his mouth. 'Upstairs, first floor, second door on the right.'

I don't often get the chance to tower over upstarts and I took full advantage of the opportunity.

'They call you kid because you're nothing but a loud-mouthed squirt?' I enquired casually.

The kid looked daggers at me.

'I'll getcha,' he replied hotly. 'Jist you see 'f I don't. I'll getcha 'f it's the last fing I ever do.'

I grinned at him hugely.

'Sure you will, kid.'

140

'Yuh best shoot orf while yuh got the chance,' the big man said. 'The kid's a terror when 'e's roused.'

I gave the kid a cheeky wink and bounded up the stairs. The kid looked daggers at me all the way up to the first floor.

Len Stokes, the professional minder, was hanging about on the landing. He came striding towards me with his face twisted into something that might've been a smile.

'Stone me, Ed,' he whispered, 'where the 'ell yuh bin? Willy's bin waitin' on yuh fer 'ours.' He jabbed a stubby finger along the landing. 'We captured the geezer wot's bin bumpin' orf the upper classes.'

'Lead me to him,' I said.

Len walked a short distance back along the corridor and paused in front of a door numbered with a brass 4. He braced himself a little, raised a clenched fist and pounded on the door three times, paused, pounded twice, paused, pounded once. A key turned in the lock on the inside and the door opened a crack. An eye appeared in the crack and gunned us for several seconds, then the door swung open and I went inside.

It was a largish room, full of ugly Victorian furniture. The heavy brocade curtains were tightly drawn and not a chink of daylight filtered into the room. Half a dozen naked light bulbs glared in a hideous *art nouveau* chandelier from the ceiling. Bound securely, with stout hemp rope, to an elaborately carved wooden armchair, directly beneath the chandelier was a grey-haired, grim-faced army sergeant with a chest full of medal ribbons. He was flanked by a couple of unpleasant-looking individuals with whom no law-abiding citizen would care to be seen dead.

There were other gorillas dotted here and there around the room. Lounging in an armchair, upholstered in black leather, by the fireplace was Willy Paradis. He got to his feet, mustered a smile and wrung my hand warmly as I drew abreast of him. But he looked like a man with perilous problems on his mind.

'Fine mess yuh got me inter,' he said, placing an arm around my shoulder and promenading me to a secluded corner of the room.

I said: 'Do me a favour, Willy. You rowed yourself in on this lark and you can't deny it.'

141

'Don't remind me,' he replied, hopelessly. 'Don't remind me.'

I glanced over my shoulder at the sergeant.

'There won't half be a scream at the War Office when they find out you're kidnapping members of the armed forces,' I said. 'How much ransom you asking?'

'Don't take the piss,' said Willy. 'The boys seen 'im creepin' outta the Peverils' Belgravia gaff. 'E 'ad it away in an army motor an' the boys tailed 'im down 'ere. 'E was rentin' this room. Any old 'ow all we've got outta 'im so far is 'is name, rank and bleedin' serial number.'

I let out an involuntary yelp of laughter.

'What did he say his name was?'

'Why don'tcha arst 'im yuhself?' said Willy. ' 'E wouldn't come 'is guts even when Greasy Thumb Tom threatened to pull 'is finger nails out.'

I marched resolutely to the centre of the room. The sergeant glared up at me defiantly. His face was bright red and contrasted sharply with his hair; his eyes were steely blue and his jaw looked as though it'd been carved out of granite. I'd seen him before.

Even trussed up there was no mistaking his military bearing. He looked like a man accustomed to obeying orders without question.

I straightened my back and barked: 'Name, rank and serial number, soldier.'

'Frederick Parkhurst, 7864 stroke 24159, sergeant, second battalion, Coldstream Guards, sah!' he clipped, then pursed his lips as though they'd been sealed with glue.

'Sounds like a bleedin' alias to me,' sneered one of the tearaways.

Willy strolled over and stood at my side.

'Ain't Parkhurst the name of the butler wot got done in in the first place?' he asked.

I said: 'That's right.'

Willy said: 'Wot the 'ell 'e doin' 'ere then?'

'Don't ask me,' I said. 'Ask him.'

Willy grinned at the sergeant.

'Wotcha doin' 'ere when yuh s'posed to 'a' bin bumped orf?'

142

'Frederick Parkhurst, 7864 stroke 24159, sergeant, second battalion, Coldstream Guards.'

'How long have you had him tied up?' I asked.

'More or less since we captured 'im,' said Willy. 'Didn't wonna take no chance on 'im doin' a scarper.'

I gave the sergeant a winning smile and said: 'If I untie you will you give me your word that you won't try to escape?'

'It is the duty of a prisoner of war to try to escape,' he replied. 'But you have my word, sah.'

I glanced at Willy.

'Okay?'

He nodded.

'Suitcha self, but if 'e slips froo our fingers it's down to you, right?'

I went around behind the chair and began unpicking the knots. Willy's team of villains looked far from happy. They stood around baring their teeth and frowning. They made no effort to help me untie the ropes.

Parkhurst eased himself out of the chair and stamped his hob-nailed boots on the floor to get the blood circulating in his legs.

'You all right, sergeant Parkhurst?' I enquired respectfully.

'Remarkably good order, sah.' He came smartly to attention and cast a disdainful eye over Willy's band of hooligans.

'Shower,' he snorted, 'never seen such a shower in my life. Not one of 'em would last five minutes on the parade ground.'

The tearaways shuffled their feet.

'Would you like a drink?' I asked.

'Pint of bitter, sah.'

I glanced at Willy and Willy glanced at the heavy on the door.

'Wotcha waitin' for, Blue Boy? Shoot down the bar and get the sergeant a pinta wallop.'

Blue Boy grunted and went out.

I offered Parkhurst a cigarette. He raised a reproving hand and gravely shook his head.

'Don't smoke, sah,' he said. 'Prefer to keep myself in the peak of physical condition.'

'Quite right, sergeant.' I lit a cigarette and blew a cloud of smoke into the air. 'Fit enough to answer a few questions?'

'Fire away, sah!'

143

I glanced at Willy; Greasy Thumb glanced at his colleagues. Everyone glanced at everyone else in complete astonishment.

'Is it you who has been going around murdering people?' I asked.

Parkhurst said: 'Honour of the regiment and the Peveril family name was at stake, sah.'

I said: 'What do you mean exactly?'

'Indelicate matter, sah,' he replied gravely. 'His lordship was a fine solider and a credit to the regiment, sah. Until his recent financial troubles. I felt it was my duty to protect the good name of the Peveril family and the regiment – I have been in Sir Samford's service for more than twenty years. We were side by side through many campaigns during the Korean conflict, sah.'

'Was that his body I found lying about in the drawing-room?'

'Alas it was, sah.'

'But how did he come to be wearing your clothes?'

His face contorted with rage. He was about to reply when suddenly the door flew open and Blue Boy came in with his hands in the air; he was followed by the bellicose little fighting cock I'd had a run in with down in the bar, also with his hands up. Behind him came the big man with his hands up and finally with his hands up came Len Stokes.

Lady Sonia brought up the rear with the pearl-handled pistol clasped resolutely in her dainty mitt.

CHAPTER THIRTY

There was a scuffle, the gun went off and the hideous *Art Nouveau* chandelier shattered into a thousand pieces. It was no loss to our national heritage. The room was plunged into darkness.

There were too many people milling about anyway. With the lights out, pandemonium broke loose. Everyone started falling over each other and swearing. Willy's voice barked loudly above the din:

'Don't let the bleeders get away!'

Then some bright spark drew the curtains and the room was bathed in sunlight.

Greasy Thumb Tom had Sonia in a half nelson – she was blistering with indignation and giving a virtuoso performance in fishwife invective. Two other tearaways had claimed hold of Parkhurst and were clinging to him for dear life as he charged about like an enraged bull. For some reason Willy was all of a heap on the floor. He picked himself up, dusted himself off and regained his dignity by doing his nut.

'I fortcha was s'posed to be mindin' the soddin' door,' he snarled at Blue Boy.

Blue Boy's cheeks turned pink.

'Told me to get the beer, didn'tcha guv?'

'Door minders are s'posed to turn the twirl in the lock when they go out.'

'Forgot,' said Blue Boy.

'I'm surrounded by a shower of bleedin' idiots,' Willy groaned.

'Good morning, your ladyship,' pronounced Parkhurst sonorously. 'I am somewhat incommoded at the moment, but may I offer you a chair?'

'Don't let that man come near me,' shrieked Sonia.

The two heavies tightened their grip.

'Greasy Thumb,' said Willy. 'Where's yuh manners. Tie 'er ladyship to a chair.'

'Sorry, guv, I wasn't fingkin'.'

Willy turned to me: 'I reckon it's 'igh time we got this caper sorted out once an' for all, Ed. I've gotta sneakin' sus these two can mark our card about the whole fing. My boys can get anyfing out of anyone if they set their minds to it.'

'Let's give it a whirl,' I agreed.

Willy swivelled his black leather chair to face the culprits. Trying to negotiate a favourable self-image, Parkhurst stood stiffly to attention with his nose in the air while Sonia, dishevelled and bloodshot, was trying to persuade Greasy Thumb Tom to get her hip flask out of her purse and give her a belt. It turned out to be empty.

I perched on the arm of Willy's chair.

Speaking politely Willy addressed Sonia: 'Now, yuh ladyship, we'd like to 'ear wot you two 'ave been doing' of. Uvva wise ole

Greasy Thumb 'ere is gonna 'ave to bust a few fingers an' knee caps and fings around 'ere.'

Lady Sonia kicked her shapely legs wildly and tried to break out of the chair.

'He did it,' she screamed. 'He did it all. He murdered Samford and Patrick . . . and he was going to murder me as well. All I wanted was to stop him . . . that's the only reason I came here.'

'Calm yourself, your ladyship,' barked Parkhurst. 'You have a stay of execution, but no more. Your crimes are such that a soldier must answer with his life. The firing squad at dawn.'

''E's orf 'is rocker,' whispered Willy.

I nodded and addressed Parkhurst in the authoritative voice of an officer and a gentleman:

'Sergeant Parkhurst, I would be grateful if you would give me a full report on the death of Sir Samford Peveril.'

'Sah,' bawled Parkhurst, apparently agreeing to the suggestion and coming even more stiffly to attention, if that were possible. Then he drew in a lung-full of air and let rip with an avalanche of raw deeds.

'At four hundred hours on Wednesday the thirteenth of June . . .'

'That'd be ten days ago,' murmured Willy.

'. . . Major Peveril called me to the drawing-room and issued me with orders – they were orders with which no soldier in Her Majesty's army could comply, sah . . .'

I coaxed him on with an encouraging nod.

'. . . A few days previously I had been fortunate enough to apprehend a burglar in the act of removing the Peveril jewels from the Major's wall safe. The Major remonstrated with me over this. He told me that a certain Mr Diamonds Silverman had been instructed to remove these jewels and that they would in turn be placed secretly in my hands and that I should smuggle them behind enemy lines for the purpose of sale. It was a strategy which I could not condone, sah.'

He regarded me anxiously, apparently hoping that I would excuse this act of insubordination.

'You acted most correctly, sergeant,' I assured him, in what I hoped was a military tone. 'Please continue.'

'I understand, sah, that Mr Silverman had been introduced to the Major by a certain Miss Pride, a woman of low breeding and criminal connections, with whom the Major was besotted, sah.'

A brutal expression took possession of Willy's face and he leapt from his chair.

'Yuh'll take that back, yuh murderin' bastard,' he hollered. 'Blue Boy, fill 'im in.'

'No, no,' I yelped, laying a restraining hand on Willy's arm. 'He's a raving nut-case anyway, but he's singing like a canary. If you kick his teeth down his throat he won't be able to tell us any more.'

Willy subsided and called off Blue Boy whose fist was already raised and glinting with a knuckle duster.

I turned to Parkhurst, trying to resume my military bearing.

'Control your language, sergeant. Miss Pride is an extremely respectable girl – she is the daughter of Mr Paradis here.'

'Sah!' he returned predictably.

'You remonstrated with the Major over this suggestion, I assume, sergeant?' I continued encouragingly.

'I did remonstrate with him, sah. I refused to obey his orders. The jewels were family heirlooms, you understand, sah. The Major held them in trust for his nephew, Mr James Davenport.'

'Then what happened?'

Willy's team had now formed a semi-circle around Parkhurst and were gaping at him in open admiration. The code to which a soldier holds firm differed little to that of the underworld, it would seem.

'The Major drew a gun on me, sah. It was a case of court martial . . . He was dishonouring the regiment. But . . . we had been through the war together, fought side by side in the jungle, sah . . .' Parkhurst's tone was changing. He was beginning to sound wretched, almost human. I thought I detected a catch in his throat. 'He had always treated me as a comrade in arms. It was wrong, I know, but I felt that I must show him mercy. A private execution would spare him public disgrace.'

'Yuh did 'im a favour,' Blue Boy put in and the rest of the tearaways nodded their profound agreement.

'How did you do it?' I asked.

'I am trained in unarmed combat, sah. He pulled the trigger as I jumped him, but he was off balance and the shot went wild. It was quick and merciful, sah, a single well-aimed karate chop and he fell dead at my feet.'

The tearaways sent up a cheer.

I said firmly, 'Where does her ladyship come into it, sergeant?'

'Lady Sonia and Mr Tomlinson entered the room just as the Major joined his noble ancestors. They must have heard the gun go off.'

'It's a lie,' screamed Sonia. 'It's all lies from beginning to end . . .'

'Put a sock in it, yuh ladyship,' grunted Greasy Thumb Tom.

'Her ladyship perpetrated a deception. She persuaded me that the honour of the regiment would be tarnished for ever if it became too widely known that I had summarily executed my commanding officer. Mr Tomlinson gave me a substantial sum of money to leave the country.'

'Least 'e coulda done,' said Len Stokes.

'Why didn't you go?' I queried.

I could not leave England, sah,' Parkhurst actually trembled, 'without bidding adieu to my old barracks at Aldershot. I had a drink in the sergeant's mess and intended to spend my last night in the country at this hostelry.' His brow darkened. 'The following morning, as I was about to set off for one of the coastal towns, I happened to buy a newspaper, sah. I found myself reading of my own murder. You will understand I'm sure that I was much affected. And it did not take me long to realize that the Major's corpse had been indecorously reclothed in my butler's uniform, sah. The Major and I were exactly the same size and build, you see. His countenance had been lacerated with a fire iron. It was conduct unbecoming – no soldier could condone it. It was imperative upon me to see to the execution of those who would further defile the honour of the Coldstream Guards . . . I refer to her ladyship and Mr Tomlinson, sah.'

'Wot's 'e on about?' Len Stokes blurted out.

'They bashed in the Major's boat race so's the law'd fink it was ole Park'urst wot got dun in – 'stead of the uvver way round, yuh burk,' Blue Boy explained.

'Dead cunnin' that was,' Len agreed. 'But couldn't the law 'ave taken 'is dabs and tumbled 'oo it was that way?'

'They could have,' I put in. 'But they don't usually keep finger prints of the aristocracy at the Yard.'

'Stone me, I fort they 'ad everyone's dabs on file.'

'If you never get nicked for anything you never have your finger prints taken.'

'There ain't no one in this world don't get their collar felt sometime or uvver,' Len replied adamantly.

Further explanation would've been futile so I dropped the matter.

'He was out to kill me . . . I told you so,' sobbed Lady Sonia.

'No you didn't,' I corrected her. 'You said that it was Sir Samford who was going to kill you.'

'What'sh the difference,' she choked.

'Better get her a shot of brandy,' I advised Greasy Thumb. 'We want her side of the story before she falls apart.'

'I ain't runnin' errands for a bird wot bashes 'er old man's boat in wiv a poker after 'e's snuffed it,' said Greasy Thumb.

'Do like 'e says,' snapped Willy. 'I don't wonna 'ang about 'ere all day.'

Greasy Thumb Tom headed reluctantly towards the door, and his mumbled complaints drifted up to us as he made his way downstairs: 'Cavin' yuh old man's skull when 'e's up an' about is one fing, but when 'e's dead as mutton ain't fair . . .' He returned shortly with a bottle of Martell and a wine-glass. He filled the glass and held it to her lips.

'Thankyoushomuch,' she gasped and drank greedily. 'Can I have shum more?' she asked when it was empty.

''Old it,' said Willy. 'What was the idea of gettin' yuh 'usband up in yuh butler's kit, Lady Sonia? Yuh can 'ave anuvver swig when yuh told us.'

She looked around at the collection of ugly mugs, in the hope of finding one with a trace of sympathy in it. She had no luck and started to sob again.

'Patrick, Patrick! How could you leave me? I can't face it without you!'

'Hold on.' I gave Willy a quick glance. 'Tomlinson was blackmailing Samford, right?'

Willy nodded.

'Pru says so – so wot?'

149

'So, with Samford out of the way, the whole shooting match is supposed to pass to Elinor's son James.'

'Elinor'sh a bish,' snarled Sonia. 'She never think'sh of anyshing but her shtupid shon. How dare she arsh to shee the deedsh to Bramley? A poor relashion arshing to shee the deedsh! I never heard anything sho rediculush – why should we show them to her?'

I suddenly had what felt like a flash of insight.

'You and Tomlinson had put your heads together and transferred the deeds into his name, hadn't you?' I asked.

'Never shaid sho – what'sh it got to do with you anyway?' She was drunk as a coot and I feared that at any moment she would pass out.

I talked fast.

'You see! They'd got their mitts on the deeds to Bramley Hall and probably plenty of other stuff as well which James would expect to come into. With Samford dead, the solicitors would've got going on the estate and the whole little caper would've come to light. They couldn't afford to let Samford die, especially when they found him dead. So they just switched the identity of the corpse. Risky game, I'll grant you, but they had a lot to lose and stood a good chance of ending up in the number one court at the Old Bailey for fraud. So they had to keep up the fiction of Samford being alive. They had to invent all kinds of stories like the one about his turning up at Bramley.'

'Dishonour,' groaned Parkhurst. 'Is there no end to this dishonour?'

Willy gave me a wink and smiled broadly.

'I like it,' he chuckled. 'It's beginning to add up.'

I pressed on.

'Then the sergeant here bumped off Tomlinson.' I was really inspired now. 'I suppose you saw that too, didn't you?' I gave Sonia a sidelong glance.

'He shmurdered Patrick . . .'

'Shmurdered!' echoed Willy's henchmen and roared with laughter.

Sonia slouched in her chair with her head bent and her hair falling over her face. I nudged Greasy Thumb and told him to

150

give her a spot more brandy. He stuck the bottle in her mouth and she gulped some down.

'I shaw it,' she gasped. 'I ran and ran. He wash going to murder me . . . I shaw it in hish eyesh . . . sho I ran and ran.' I'd heard this side of the record before; I wanted to hear what was on the other side.

'Right,' I said. 'Now let's get down to cases about the jewels. Did you hide them in the bust of Shelley, sergeant?'

'Certainly not, sah,' he retorted contemptuously.

Willy pointed an accusing finger at Lady Sonia.

'She mustta put 'em there,' he bawled triumphantly. Willy was a man of action, he didn't like sitting around for long periods and was eager to be on his way.

'Jamesh shan't have them,' screeched Sonia wildly.

'That's right,' I agreed. 'So you and Patrick stuck them in the bust of Shelley. You busted into your own wall safe so's it'd look like burglary – it would be easy to come back and pocket the jewels at your leisure.'

The look Sonia gave me was enough to drive anyone to drink.

'Patrick shaw you climb out the back window,' she hissed. 'Patrick shaw you. He knew who'd taken the jewels.'

'Where are they now?' asked Willy, quick as a flash.

'I think I might elucidate that, sah,' Parkhurst said quietly.

All eyes in the room turned upon him.

'Get elucidatin', sarge,' snapped Willy.

'At the time of the execution of Mr Tomlinson, he had the Peveril jewels on his person, sah.' He was speaking to me again. He'd definitely decided that I was officer material.

'Very good, sergeant,' I clipped. I'd nursed him along so far there was no point in not playing him along the rest of the way. 'What happened?'

'I was paying a visit to London, sah. Undercover you understand. Doing a reckie of the Peveril residence in Belgravia. There was a commando raid planned . . .' He glanced around at the sea of interested faces. ' . . . but that's top secret.'

'Shame,' sighed Len.

'Passing down Piccadilly I came face to face with my sister, Gloria. Her name is . . .'

151

'Gloria Ra. . . .' I silenced Blue Boy with a sharp kick on the shin.

Parkhurst continued:

'She seemed surprised to see me, so I explained to her what had been happening and informed her that my present billet was in Aldershot. Even scribbled down the address on a slip of paper for her.'

'You trusted your sister, no doubt,' I said encouragingly.

Parkhurst nodded gloomily.

'The following evening, I returned to my billet to find that the place had been broken into. At first, I couldn't understand it. Then I discovered that the Peveril jewels were missing. Amongst the debris I subsequently found the slip of paper on which I had written the address for my sister. I was cast down, sah, ashamed and cast down.'

Willy spoke for us all:

'It's a diabolical liberty when yuh can't even trust yuh own skin and blister.'

'I returned to town immediately and sought out my sister and discovered to my horror and disgust that she was consorting with a bad man from the lower classes. Mr Silverman, the very same bounder whose henchman I'd surprised attempting to remove the gems from the Major's safe a week or two previously . . .'

'So you done 'im in and took the tomfoolery back?' Willy snapped impatiently.

'No, sah.' A mad look came into Parkhurst's eyes. 'I gave it to the gal straight. Mr Silverman must be liquidated. Either she would undertake the assignment herself, in which case I would excuse her fall from grace. Or she must suffer with him at my hands.'

'So she gave it to 'im wiv the dagger between the shoulder blades, right?' said Willy sadly. 'Diamonds was the finest fence that ever lived. We won't see the likes of 'im again.'

'Naturally,' said Parkhurst. 'Gloria complied with my wishes and returned the jewels to me. If you look in the drawer of that desk over there you will find them.' He nodded towards the far corner of the room.

Half a dozen pairs of horny hands started clutching at the

drawer handles. There was so much pushing and shoving that it was a full minute before the firm got it open.

Willy eased himself out of his chair and strolled over to the fringes of the mob.

'Stand aside,' he ordered and they meekly made way for him. Willy reached into the drawer and came up with a familiar black velvet bag between his forefinger and thumb. He returned to his chair and spilt the contents out onto a table. I recognized the sparklers that I'd last seen in my office.

The glitter woke Sonia up.

'They're mine,' she shrilled. 'They're mine.'

Willy fingered one sparkling piece after another with greedy admiration.

'Not any more, they're not, lady,' he said.

In the distance came the wail of a police siren. It was the sort of sound that the sort of people in that room picked up like hound dogs.

'Stone me!' shouted Len. 'It's the filth.'

I cast my eyes to the ground with embarrassment.

'Sorry, fellers,' I confessed. 'I forgot to mention I phoned the law from the motorway garage and put them in the picture.'

'Wotcha wanna go an' do a silly fing like that for?'

I said: 'I wasn't thinking.'

'Everyone out,' ordered Willy. 'Out the back way on the hurry up.' Parkhurst made as if to follow the firm as they dashed out of the door. Willy pointed the pearl-handled revolver at him. 'Not you, sunshine – stick 'em mitts up.'

Parkhurst retraced his steps with his hands in the air.

'Looks like this is your collar, Ed,' smiled Willy. 'All yuh gotta do is keep 'em covered 'til Clews shows. Yuh'll be a bleedin' 'ero when yuh tell all about 'ow yuh captured the most wanted man in England all on yuh tod and 'er ladyship thrown in for good measure.' He strolled over to the door. 'Be seein' yuh, loser.'

'Now hold on there,' I bleated. 'You can't leave me alone with these desperate criminals ... I don't like guns, they make too much noise. Come back, Willy! Come back!' But he was gone and the roar of several high-powered get-away cars was receding into the distance.